Sutherland's PRIDE

Kathryn Brocato, author of *Old Christmas*

CRIMSON ROMANCE

F+W Media, Inc.

Published by
Crimson Romance
an imprint of F+W Media, Inc.
10151 Carver Road, Suite 200
Blue Ash, Ohio 45242

www.crimsonromance.com

This is a work of fiction. Names, characters, corporations, institutions, organizations, events, or locales in this novel are either the product of the author's imagination or, if real, used fictitiously. The resemblance of any character to actual persons (living or dead) is entirely coincidental.

Dedication

This book is dedicated to my childhood friends:

Nancy DuBose Richardson
and
Peggy "Jolene" Jordan Kenyon

Chapter One

"What on earth are you reading?" Flynn Sutherland asked. In less than five hours, he would see Pride Donovan again for the first time in three years, and he wanted to get an early start on the work that awaited him.

His secretary, Killeen Ross, buried in the depths of the *Houston Chronicle*, appeared to be sinking deeper by the minute as she thumbed through section after section.

"I'm looking for my favorite column." Killeen's brown pageboy appeared for a moment above the sheets of newsprint. "This is Thursday. Tracy Eric's 'Single Mommy' column is supposed to be—here it is. They keep moving it."

"'Single Mommy?'" Flynn repeated, in tones of distaste. He leaned over Killeen from behind her chair so that his sun-bleached, dark blond hair almost brushed her cheek.

"It's a fantastic column," Killeen said. "She writes about single parenting, all the way from having the baby on your own to how it feels to have a date for the first time in two years. She gives hints on how to cope and tells you how much to pay the baby sitter— everything a woman in my situation needs to know."

Flynn raised his brows but wisely said nothing. Killeen had just been liberated from a bad marriage, thanks to Flynn's legal expertise, and was rearing two teenagers by herself.

Killeen folded the paper open and spread it out on her desk. "I know several single fathers who keep up with Tracy's column. There's no one else they can turn to."

Flynn bent further over Killeen's desk and studied the column. Above the title, "When You Have to Go Home Again," a photograph of an attractive, dark-haired woman caught his eye.

"Oh, wow," Killeen muttered. "She's going back home for the first time in three years. That's where it all happened."

"What happened?" Flynn asked.

"Tracy Eric got pregnant three years ago, but her boyfriend deserted her. Now she's coming home for the first time in three years. She's going to fill us in on what it feels like."

Flynn experienced a momentary jolt. Three years ago, Pride Donovan had faced him in her Houston apartment, told him she was pregnant, and asked him what he wanted to do about it. He had stalled. The baby could not have been his, as doctors had pronounced him sterile since a bad case of childhood measles. But before he could give in and marry her, Pride had disappeared.

"She ought to leave well enough alone," Flynn observed.

"Not Tracy. That's the beauty of this column. You feel as if Tracy Eric is your best friend, and the two of you are talking over cups of coffee at the kitchen table."

"That good, huh?"

Flynn never read over his secretary's shoulder, but this aroused his interest. Pride Donovan had been gifted in writing pieces that made you feel you were inside her heart. He stood behind Killeen and swiftly absorbed the column.

He found the premise simple enough. Tracy Eric, a young, single mother, was returning to her Texas hometown for the first time in three years to bury her father, who had disowned Tracy when she became pregnant out of wedlock. Future columns would fill the readers in on Tracy's feelings about reliving old memories and renewing old acquaintances with her son in tow.

He suppressed a mild sense of surprise. Pride was coming home to bury her father also, but without a son in tow.

He wished suddenly with all his heart that Pride had married him and borne a son after all. The baby would be his.

Flynn straightened, shaking his head. People ought not to dwell on the past. Talk about an unproductive pastime....

"This column is so popular, the *Chronicle* started running it twice a week," Killeen said. "Do you know what that means?"

"I'm afraid to ask," Flynn said. "However, I have to attend a funeral at two o'clock. Are those letters ready to sign?"

"Give me five minutes, boss." Killeen skimmed the column.

Flynn smiled. Killeen had probably stayed overtime yesterday to type the letters. His instincts had not betrayed him when he had hired her and acted in her behalf in court. She was a loyal secretary who always put his interests first in the office.

He went into his office and stared out the windows at the Houston skyline. Too bad his instincts were so off target when he became involved with Pride Donovan. He would never have picked Pride as a woman who would two-time a man, yet, how else could she have become pregnant?

That Pride would have tried to trick him into marriage by the oldest scam around still shocked him. Her pale face and hurt green eyes almost coaxed him into forgetting that he was a rich man's son, a target for hundreds of marriage-minded women.

He turned away from the window and picked up a file folder. She vanished from Houston and the small, Southeast Texas town of Anahuac soon after he began his successful stalling procedure. Sure enough, she claimed she had miscarried soon after.

Outwardly, he professed relief, but the hurt remained. Probably what hurt worse was the fact that he missed her, longed for her, and had even gone so far as to search for her.

He should have married her anyway and claimed the baby as his own, if there had really been a baby.

Pride Donovan hadn't been spectacularly beautiful, but parts of her were definitely spectacular. She had honest green eyes, delicate, feathery brows, and a sprinkling of freckles across a lovely, straight nose. Her hair was a wild tangle of light-brown curls, and her skin sported a perpetual light tan during the months she spent with him.

Flynn smiled, remembering Pride's determination to hoist the mainsail on his sailboat by herself. The wind had been stronger than Pride, and she wound up in the water.

Pride always went after things like that, things that involved acting first and thinking later. No doubt that's that had happened when she came up with the idea of pretending pregnancy to encourage his proposal. She simply went ahead with the plan before she took the time to think it over.

Obviously, she hadn't been pregnant at all, but Flynn had passed many a lonely night thinking about the child Pride might have given birth to. Of course, there was no way he could have been the child's father, but suppose a miracle happened and the baby had resembled him?

Pulling out his chair, Flynn jerked his mind off that subject and thought about Pride. She had been special, and he had wanted to marry her, until she jumped the gun and tried to force his hand.

*

Pride Donovan suffered through her father's funeral without shedding a tear. Helping to corral four small children during the service kept her mind occupied and her sorrow tamped back.

Any private sorrow she felt would be dealt with later. That was the story of her life now, she admitted. Her own feelings came later. She would sort them out on paper, where she best dealt with everything.

The following morning she drove to Houston, accompanied by her cousin and the four small children, to learn the contents of her father's will.

Something warned her to bring her relatives for along for support. Judge Alan Donovan had been a strange and bitter man, and Pride did not put it past him to try and humiliate her one last time through his will.

"Johnny, stop that," she cried.

Johnny, two years old and full of curiosity and energy, twisted in Pride's arms. Houston traffic fascinated Johnny, and he wanted to get right out there in the middle of it. The moment his small feet touched the ground in the downtown parking garage, he made a run for the street.

"Are you sure you don't want to go alone?" her cousin, Gloria Boudreaux, asked. "In another minute, there'll be total anarchy around here. It's a shame the weather is so pretty."

Pride agreed. The late May sky glowed a deep, cloudless blue. The usual Gulf Coast humidity was temporarily absent, thanks to a cool front, and the spring foliage retained the new green color of early spring. She couldn't blame the children for wanting to make use of it.

"I'd rather you came with me," Pride said, nerves jittering. "I have a feeling I'm going to need some support."

"You call four children under the age of five support?" Gloria asked. "Eric Boudreaux, stop that this instant. Why should there be any trouble over your father's will?"

"Daddy never did anything without causing some sort of trouble. Why should his will be any different?" She could not put into words the feeling of impending disaster that hung over her.

"Now that's a reason if I ever heard one," Gloria said, grinning.

Gloria was a slender woman with wildly curling dark hair and large, brown eyes. The two-year-old girl in her arms repeated Gloria's coloring, as did the two children on the sidewalk between the two women. Pride loved them to distraction. Without them, she could not have made it through the past three years.

The fourth child, who rode in Pride's arms, also had large brown eyes, but his hair was dark blond.

"You and the children are tremendously comforting to me," Pride said. "I can't imagine going anywhere alone. I wouldn't know how to behave. This way, Tracy."

Walking down a busy, downtown Houston sidewalk carrying two small children and leading two others by the hand wasn't easy, but the women managed it.

"I know what you mean," Gloria said. "That week Eddie and I spent in New Orleans while you kept the kids nearly drove us both nuts. Too much silence. No interruptions of tender moments. No little faces to wipe."

"Exactly," Pride said. "Come on."

"Are you going to get in touch with Flynn Sutherland today?" Gloria asked in casual tones.

Pride winced inwardly and felt the jangle of all her pulses. "I'm not ready yet. I'm still considering the most distantly friendly method of contacting him."

"I thought you said you caught a glimpse of him at the funeral yesterday," Gloria said. "Don't you think he has a few questions about Johnny?"

"Like what?" Pride's voice remained cheerful in spite of her inner anguish. Flynn had not approached her to so much as offer condolences. "If he thinks about it at all, he'll figure Johnny could not possibly have anything to do with him."

"Now I would say Johnny has everything to do with Flynn Sutherland. Tracy Boudreaux, give Aunt Pride your hand. No, you can't walk by yourself. Not on these sidewalks."

"Daddy put the word out that I'd had a miscarriage the minute I left town," Pride managed to say around the lump in her throat. "No doubt Flynn found that a tremendous relief."

"I'll never understand why your father would say such a thing," Gloria marveled. "Eric, stop that. What if you'd shown back up and made a liar out of him?"

"Believe me, Gloria, the thought never crossed his mind. No one bucked Judge Donovan when he laid down the law."

"That's just plain weird." Gloria shook her head. "Johnny was his grandchild."

"Daddy was never quite certain I was his daughter." Pride hid her hurt behind a smile. "Hold still, Johnny." They stopped before one of downtown Houston's glass towers and Pride compared the numbers on the door to a paper in her hand. "This is it."

"He was," Gloria said. "He just thought he'd found a useful little item to control your mother, that's all. You look too much like him not to be his daughter."

Pride nodded and held the big glass door open for her relatives to enter. Alan Donovan had been a handsome man, with green eyes like Pride's. He had manufactured the idea that his wife had been seeing another man just before she married him, and that Pride was the other man's child rather than his own.

Pride's gentle mother had tired at last of trying to out-argue him. During the last years of her life, Mary Donovan hadn't even tried to deny it when her husband accused her of two-timing him during their engagement.

Pride hadn't let him get away with it when he'd tried to accuse her of not being his daughter. She challenged him to a DNA test, the results of which would be made public, and he shut up.

"Flynn deserves one more chance, don't you think?" Gloria urged. "From what you've said, he'll probably never father another child."

"As far as I'm concerned, Johnny is my child and no one else's," Pride stated. "No man is ever going to treat me the way my father treated my mother."

"Well, he might have changed his mind about things," Gloria said, in soothing tones. "People do change, you know."

"I doubt if Flynn has," Pride said. "Daddy probably went to his grave thinking I'm not really his daughter. I can't wait to see if he left me the proverbial penny in his will."

She pushed open another glass door that marked the building's foyer and urged Tracy to step inside. Gloria followed, leading Eric.

"I hope you know where you're going," Gloria said. "I'm a small-town girl. These Houston skyscrapers scare me."

"They're definitely no fun during a hurricane," Pride agreed. "Hold the elevator, please."

She hurried her cousin and the children onto the elevator, punched the button for the fifteenth floor, and tried to keep Tracy from wandering to the other side of the cubicle.

"I'll be glad to get back to Lake Charles," Gloria said.

Pride grinned and agreed. "Johnny Donovan, if you want me to put you down, you're going to have to hold still until I can."

The elevator stopped several times. Each time, Tracy tried to step off the elevator, and Pride blocked the little girl.

When the elevator halted at the fifteenth floor, Tracy had finally gotten the idea and refused to exit with her relatives.

"How do people stand living here?" Gloria asked.

"They lead lives of quiet desperation." Pride laughed at her cousin's comical grimace.

They marched down the hall, children in tow, until they were certain they were headed in the correct direction.

"Here we are," Pride said at last. "Suite 1542. Oh, Lord. Be still, my fluttering heart. Flynn's gotten himself an office."

Her heart didn't just flutter. It bounded, bounced and pounded. No wonder Flynn had avoided her at the funeral.

Her feeling of impending fate was right on target. Thank goodness she had paid attention to her intuition and brought Gloria and the children along.

"Flynn? Sutherland?" Gloria stared at the elegant gold letters. "I thought he worked for the family business."

"Why would Daddy leave his will with Flynn?" Pride wondered aloud. She focused all her attention on the thought and ignored the wild hope roaring through her. "He was a big one on proper appearances. He should have ignored Flynn's existence."

Gloria looked helplessly at Pride. "What are you going to do? This has got to be the world's worst timing. I mean, how do you show a man his son for the first time with your cousin and her three hyperactive youngsters looking on?"

"Are you kidding?" Pride gathered her thoughts and reminded herself not to hope. "Flynn probably believed Daddy and still thinks I had a miscarriage. Not that he'd think my son had anything to do with him, anyway," she added, for good measure.

Gloria's mouth tightened. "I'd better stay out here with the children while you go in. He might just surprise you if he doesn't have an audience."

"Maybe." Pride smiled and took firm hold of emotions. "But let's keep matters interesting. How much would you like to bet that Flynn thinks Johnny is your child rather than mine?"

"You mean you aren't going to tell him?"

"Why should I? He never made any effort to check on me, so it won't hurt him to wait until I'm ready before I tell him." She hoped her smile covered her hurt over that fact. "Tell you what. If I can sit there in Flynn's office, with Johnny on my lap, without Flynn suspecting anything, you owe me lunch."

"Pride, I hate to mention this, but Johnny doesn't look anything like me. He looks more like you, especially since you've lightened your hair."

"He looks a lot like Flynn, actually," Pride said. "Come on, Gloria. Where are your sporting instincts?"

Gloria regarded Johnny a moment. "Do you honestly believe Flynn is going to think Johnny is my son?"

"Yes." But inside, Pride prayed he saw the truth.

Gloria lifted her brows. "All right. You're on. You did say Flynn has dark blond hair, didn't you?"

"And brown eyes," Pride supplied. "If Johnny's eyes were green, I'd start totaling up the cost of our lunch."

"I can't believe you're going to do this."

"I'm just giving Flynn the opportunity to be his usual single-minded self. If he brings the matter up, then I'll say something."

Gloria nodded. "If he's anything like Johnny, I suppose I can see your point."

"Johnny takes after Flynn in more than looks," Pride agreed. "Come on. We're a few minutes late."

She glanced down at herself, thankful she wore her navy linen suit. Cool and business-like, that was the ticket. Too bad she hadn't twisted her hair up in a tight little bun.

Pride, cradling Johnny, shoved open the glass door which bore the legend: Flynn Sutherland, Attorney at Law. Inside, an efficient-looking woman with short brown hair looked up from the brief she was typing and smiled. When she saw the four children, her smile broadened.

"I'm Pride Donovan." Pride consulted a notebook she produced from her purse. "I have an appointment with the attorney at eleven o'clock."

"Yes, Miss Donovan. He's expecting you." She punched her intercom and announced Pride. "What beautiful children."

Gloria thanked her as the door to the inner office opened and Flynn Sutherland stepped out.

Pride sucked in air and clutched her son, thankful she had a soft, sweet-smelling warm child to hold while she faced Flynn for the first time in three years. How could Flynn stand there and not realize Johnny was his own son?

"Hello, Pride," Flynn said. "Come on in."

He could because when Flynn had an idea in his head, no matter how mistaken, he ignored all clues to the contrary.

Pride detected Gloria's dawning astonishment and had to bite back a wry smile that hid her own disappointment.

Flynn looked as magnificent as ever. The sight of his tall, broad-shouldered body in the dark-gray business suit still had the power to accelerate her heart and make her shiver with longing. His red tie and white shirt accentuated his tanned skin and sun-bleached hair, hair that had originally been exactly the color of Johnny's.

His straight, dark brows had drawn together as he studied her, and his brown eyes held a thoughtful look. Pride remembered the merry, teasing expression those dark eyes had once held and squashed another shiver of longing.

Flynn appeared to note the fact that Pride had brought friends. He smiled at Eric, who approached in the fearless manner of a four-year-old boy who had never known anything but love.

"Are all of you with Pride?" Flynn watched Eric, still smiling. "Ms. Ross, will you please send out for refreshments? These children look thirsty."

"I'm Eric," Eric announced. "This is my Aunt Pride, and my mother, and this is my sister, Tracy. That's Johnny, and that's Sylvia."

Pride smiled her approval. "That's very good, Eric. Now tell the nice man your last name."

That would get Flynn, Pride decided gleefully. Being described as a nice man ought to cut one of Houston's most eligible bachelors down to a proper size.

"Boudreaux," Eric supplied.

Flynn, who had always seemed singularly oblivious to his eligibility, knelt to shake Eric's hand gravely, then he stood and smiled at Gloria.

"You're Pride's cousin," he said. "I'm Flynn Sutherland. Please come in."

"It might be better if I sit out here with the children while you talk to Pride," Gloria said. "If you have anything important to discuss, things could get a little distracting."

"I doubt if Daddy's will can be classified as important." Pride winked at Gloria. "You might as well come on in. It'll be our laugh for the day."

Flynn said nothing. He stood aside and held the door while Gloria and Pride herded their charges inside his office.

Flynn's office boasted a comfortable sofa, which Gloria and

Pride both settled on, with two children between them and one on each side.

Flynn closed the door and took in the five pairs of expectant brown eyes and the single pair of wary green eyes that focused on him.

"You look like six owls on a wire," he observed.

"That's because we're all so wise," Pride intoned. With Gloria and the children present, she found herself almost able to deal with him. "Come on, Flynn. Don't keep us in suspense. We want to know if we can buy our tickets to Bermuda now, or do we have to wait a thousand years, while the penny Daddy left me accrues interest."

"Your filial respect is impressive," Flynn said.

"If I had ever developed any filial respect, no doubt it would impress me, too," Pride said, with equal dryness. "Skip the boring parts and acquaint us with the interesting stuff. The kids want to get outside and play."

"Hold your horses." Flynn walked to his desk and perched on the corner of it, studying her. "Let me look at you a minute."

Pride looked back at him, studying him in the same way he studied her. The past three years hadn't been as kind to her as they apparently had to Flynn.

"That hair color suits you," he said, at last. "I like it."

"Thank you." Pride firmly squelched the upsurge of pleasure.

"What happened to your freckles?"

"My freckles?" She blinked, surprised. "I think they just faded away. I haven't been in the sun much these past few years."

"That will have to be remedied." Flynn studied her some more. "Are you sure you don't have them covered with makeup?"

Pride refused to get into a discussion of her makeup. She said nothing and glanced meaningfully at Gloria.

Gloria widened her eyes and gave her shoulders an infinitesimal shrug.

"Hey," Pride exclaimed. "What do you think you're doing?"

While she exchanged glances with Gloria, Flynn produced a handkerchief from his pocket, dipped it in a cup of coffee sitting on his desk, then took Pride's chin in one hand and applied the wet cloth to her nose with the other.

Immediately, an ominous tickle began inside Pride's nose.

"Mine," Johnny shouted.

Pride, thoroughly flustered, grabbed for her son as he lunged for Flynn's hand. Johnny latched onto Flynn's wrist and entangled his small fingers around Flynn's gold watchband.

Flynn, startled, paused in his ministrations to Pride's nose and stared at the little boy clinging to his wrist.

Pride sneezed, a mighty sneeze that rattled her teeth and made her eyes tear.

"Bless you." Flynn passed her the handkerchief.

"Thanks a heap—*Atchoo*. Now look what you've done. *Atchoo*."

"Mine," Johnny yelled, louder.

Pride opened watery eyes. Her son danced on the edge of the sofa with both small hands outstretched, pleading at the top of his voice.

Flynn Sutherland backed up carefully and pulled his sleeve down to cover his watch. "I seem to have started something here."

"You're right. This is all your fault." Pride dried her eyes and blew her nose with relish. "Don't you know better than to wear a mariner's watch around little children? You should have taken it off as soon as we came in. They were bound to see it."

"I'm sorry," Flynn said, looking at Gloria. "I didn't realize the reaction it would cause."

Gloria's mouth opened and closed. She appeared bereft of words.

Pride wadded Flynn's handkerchief and dried her nose. Thanks to Flynn, the whole world smelled like coffee.

"You can either take it off and put it in your drawer or you can let him play with it while we're here," Pride informed Flynn. "Otherwise, you won't get a bit of business transacted."

"Give him my watch?" Flynn regarded Johnny doubtfully.

Johnny bounced up and down on the edge of the sofa with both hands outstretched, clearly a child whose life would be forever blighted if he didn't instantly receive the object of his desire. For once, Pride enjoyed the stubborn streak that would keep her son's mind fixed on Flynn's watch until he got it.

"Mine," he cried. "Mine."

"No, Johnny, it is not yours," Pride said. "It belongs to Flynn. What have I told you about things that aren't yours?"

"Mine," Johnny reiterated tearfully.

"Do you want me to take you outside and explain the matter further?" Pride asked, in a mother's rhetorical manner.

Johnny appeared likely to expire of a broken heart at any moment.

"What have you done to him, boss?" Killeen Ross entered and set a tray on Flynn's desk. "I didn't know you went in for torturing innocent little kids."

"It's the other way around," Flynn said, over Johnny's wails.

"He got a glimpse of a forbidden treat," Pride said, tongue-in-cheek. "We're lucky the others weren't sitting where they could see it."

Flynn glanced at his own wrist. "Why my watch?"

"See all those pretty little flags on the face? Kids love telling time by reading nautical flags."

"He can read nautical flags?"

"It's in his blood," Pride said, straight-faced. "Come on, Flynn. Give."

"Mine," Johnny wailed.

"Flynn's," Pride corrected.

"Flynn's," Johnny pleaded.

"How old is he?" Flynn looked toward Gloria.

Gloria made a sound indicative of someone choking to death.

"He can't be more than two." Killeen handed out glasses of soft drink.

"He was two years old on March twelfth," Pride said. "Un-wrist that watch, Flynn, or we'll be here all day." Flynn unclasped the watch, removed it from his wrist, and brought it to Johnny. Johnny's small fingers closed around it like the arms of a starfish around an oyster.

"Johnny, what do you say?" Pride asked.

"Flynn's."

"What do you say to Flynn?"

Johnny looked up at Flynn and said in a clear, childish voice, "Thank you."

"You're welcome," Flynn said.

Killeen Ross, covering her mouth with her hand, exchanged gleeful glances with Pride and backed out of the office.

Johnny got busy trying to pry the crystal off the watch so he could get to the brightly colored nautical flags on the face of the watch.

"Now, Flynn," Pride said, grinning. "Tell us all about our trip to Bermuda."

Flynn watched Johnny a moment then lifted his gaze to her. "Why didn't you get in touch with your father before he died?"

"What makes you think I didn't?" Pride asked.

"He told me as much. When I received your father's request to handle his estate, he was in the hospital in bad shape. Before I could get there the next morning, he died."

"That's too bad," Pride said. "Obviously, he was about to make an Interesting Revelation."

"Don't be flippant." Flynn regarded her, frowning. "You've never been close to your father, have you?"

She had never told Flynn any of her troubles with her father on the grounds that people who detailed their innermost pain to other human beings were deadly bores.

"That's probably the understatement of the year," she replied. "He has always believed I'm not his real daughter."

Flynn's brown eyes went wide. He stared at her a moment in astonished silence.

"He never gave my mother a moment's peace, and he was rude and disrespectful to her in public," Pride went on. "No, I was not close to him. To tell you the truth, I didn't like him much. Therefore, I haven't any more idea than you have as to what he wanted to see you about."

"I didn't know," Flynn said, still staring.

Pride smiled. "Now, Flynn, one doesn't spill the more yucky parts of her personal history to a man unless she wants to either put him to sleep or run him off."

"I suppose you mean reserve is more interesting than excess openness." Flynn glanced behind him, picked up a folder from a stack on his desk, and turned back to face her. "I'll say this for you. You were never boring."

"Thank you." She gripped her hands together in her lap and maintained her bright smile.

He eyed her. "Your sarcasm is well-taken. Let's get down to business, before that one," he indicated Johnny, "figures out how to take my watch apart."

"He's only dismantled the clasp so far," Pride said, in comforting tones. "It'll be a while before he figures out how to scatter the little gears and gizmos all over the room."

Flynn winced. "Thanks. I needed that." He opened the folder. "To make things simple, your father died a wealthy man. He has left you his entire estate, except for a few minor bequests to distant relatives."

Pride suspected her father of trying to mess with her mind from the grave. Her parents had been well-off, but not rich by any means. She grew up in a large, brick home as befitted the daughter of a judge, and she had even received a car for her sixteenth birthday. But so had some of her friends, whose parents had big mortgages and were in hock to the local car dealership.

"That's nice." She glanced at Gloria. "Let's get packed. Maybe we can catch a flight to Bermuda late this afternoon."

Gloria hadn't taken her eyes off Flynn. She nodded and kept her mouth shut.

"Mine," Johnny said, with satisfaction.

Pride glanced down in time to see Johnny pop something into his mouth and swallow it. She grabbed for the watch, but it was too late.

"Uh-oh." She noted her son's angelic face. "You'd better take your watch back, Flynn. I do believe he ate the stem."

Flynn received the watch with disbelief.

"And," Pride added, "if I hear one word out of you about paying for repairs, I'll see to it that you get the bill for having Johnny's little stomach pumped."

Chapter Two

"Having his stomach pumped?" Flynn said. "It was only a watch stem. His digestive system will probably never notice it."

"What do you know about little children?" Pride asked. "For all we know, that watch stem could be working its deadly way into his intestines, where it will next enter his bloodstream and migrate directly to his—"

"All right," Flynn interrupted. He stared at his watch. "Let's get him X-rayed. Never let it be said that I caused the death of an innocent child."

Pride felt satisfied. She had no intention of getting Johnny X-rayed for ingesting a mere watch stem, not when he'd successfully dealt with such large items as pennies and quarters. She just thought it was high time Flynn worried a little over his own son.

Johnny climbed carefully off the sofa and toddled across the small expanse of gray carpet toward Flynn. He held up his small hands. "Flynn's."

"How do you like that?" Flynn asked. "He wants to eat the rest of it."

"Flynn's," Johnny begged.

Eric, Tracy, and Sylvia had so far behaved like model children, much to Pride's secret chagrin. Once Johnny left the sofa, they realized there were more exciting things in the office than the soft drinks in their hands.

"Oh, no." Gloria received a liberal dose of cola in her lap. "Pride, I'd better take the kids back to the car. Things are about to go downhill in a really big way." She grabbed for Sylvia, who had tumbled off the sofa to join Johnny in begging for the return of the watch. This signaled Eric to hit Tracy.

"Sylvia Boudreaux, you come back here. Eric. Tracy."

"Whoops. Well, Flynn, it's nice seeing you again." Pride almost fainted with relief. "However, all good things must end." She scooped up Johnny and Sylvia with profound gratitude. "If I need to sign anything, just put the pen between my fingers."

"Wait a minute, Pride. I wanted to take you to lunch. That's why I asked you to come in at eleven." Flynn absently re-clasped his watch. "You're all bound to be hungry."

"Not today, thank you." Pride banished the traitorous longing and smiled firmly. "If we don't get the kids home, you won't have an office. Johnny, if I hear one more word out of you about that watch, you and I will have a discussion outside."

Johnny set up a preliminary protest.

"I mean it," Pride said.

Johnny knew that tone and respected it. He shut up.

Flynn smiled. "In that case, I'll pick you up tonight. We'll have dinner. Is seven okay?"

She knew better than to fall for this, no matter how her unruly heart behaved. "Flynn, I do not have time for dinner with you. I'm only going to be in the area a few days, and I'll be busy the entire time. But I do appreciate the thought."

"Nonsense," Flynn said. "You have to eat. Besides, I need to finish telling you about your inheritance."

"You'd better go, Pride," Gloria said. "I told you this would be an impossible proposition if we brought the children."

Pride gave Gloria a look that said, "Traitor," and returned her attention to Flynn.

"Is seven all right?" Flynn repeated, smiling at Gloria.

"Seven is fine," Pride said, at last. "Johnny, stop that." She turned Sylvia over to Gloria and resettled Johnny in her arms. "No, you are not going to walk. You are going to let me carry you to the car. There will be no further discussion."

She turned toward the door, forcibly restraining her son from leaping out of her arms.

"Wear something sexy," Flynn said, laughing.

Pride halted in the door and smiled over her shoulder at him.

"What you see is what you get, and you'll be lucky if you get something that looks this good by tonight."

He had no idea, Pride thought. Her relief at escaping Flynn's office reversed to a crazy mix of joy and frustration as she looked from Flynn's face to the little face in her arms that resembled him so much.

Gloria collected her other two children and led the way to the door. "Tracy. Eric. Stop that fighting this minute, or we'll take a detour by the restroom."

"Tracy Eric," Killeen Ross said, as the two women emerged into the main office, children in tow. "She's my favorite columnist."

Gloria started but covered it well by turning to smile at Killeen. "Mine, too. I'm a happily married woman, but my husband works offshore two weeks out of every month."

"I'm newly divorced," Killeen said. "If it weren't for Tracy Eric, I don't know what I'd do."

Eric let out a terrible shout and tried to dart around his mother's legs to deal with his sister.

"Tracy Boudreaux, I'm going to have a little talk with you just as soon as we get outside this door," Gloria said sternly. "Excuse me, please. Duty calls."

Tracy, who knew punishment for socking her brother in the stomach approached, sent up a series of tearful promises.

Pride grinned at Killeen as she prepared to follow Gloria out the door. "Perhaps Tracy Eric will cover child discipline in an upcoming column."

"Let's hope," Killeen said. "I could sure use some pointers."

"Seven o'clock," Flynn said, from the door of his office.

"You may regret this." Pride gripped Eric's hand. "I intend to follow the state of Johnny's stomach very carefully this afternoon."

"If you should recover my watch stem," Flynn said, grinning, "kindly save it."

Pride exited. Flynn had definitely gotten in the last line as far as she was concerned.

*

Flynn watched as Pride Donovan walked out, leading one child by the hand and balancing the other on her hip. He found himself filled with a variety of emotions, but chief among them was the certainty that three years ago he had made a ghastly mistake.

"That's really something," Killeen said. "Two kids named Tracy and Eric. What a coincidence."

Just outside the door, Gloria Boudreaux explained to Tracy that little girls did not sock their brothers in the stomach, especially in public. The sounds of discipline being enforced made Flynn wince.

"There are lots of Tracys and Erics these days," he said absently.

He wondered what name Pride would have chosen for her child, had she carried it to term. Would it have been a boy or a girl?

He shook off the questions with impatience. It did him no good to torment himself by wondering if things would have been different had he married Pride.

The fact remained, he hadn't married Pride. He had let her get away, when he could have married her and claimed her baby as his own.

If he'd married Pride, would she have carried the child to term? If she'd been happy and secure...

He brought his thoughts to another halt. Just because Pride looked paler, thinner, and a little more strained than he remembered ever seeing her look, didn't mean she wasn't happy now. He'd better remember that.

Besides, she probably hadn't been pregnant at all. That was the first thing he'd better remember.

Flynn straightened in bitter frustration. Being sterile had never bothered him until he met Pride Donovan. Then, he'd begun thinking of marriage and children, only to find the whole thing blowing up in his face.

Today, watching Pride as she helped look after her cousin's children, he wondered what kind of mother she would have been to her own child. She had certainly managed the outspoken little blond boy well, and Flynn didn't require any experience with children to know that particular child was a handful.

Outside the door, Tracy's sobs faded into the distance. Flynn crossed the room and opened the door. Pride and Gloria were herding the children down the hall toward the elevators.

"Flynn's," Johnny cried.

Flynn grinned. Johnny, looking back over Pride's shoulder, had spotted the owner of the coveted mariner's watch at once.

Pride turned and waved, then spoke to Johnny. Johnny subsided.

Still smiling, Flynn shut the door.

"Now Pride Donovan is what I call a beautiful woman." Killeen propped her chin on her hand and regarded him. "Down-to-earth, too, and good with children."

Flynn forced a smile. Killeen definitely didn't approve of some of the women he'd been dating.

"Yes, she is. They're both beautiful women," he said, in his most noncommittal tones.

"Pride is just your type, boss," Killeen said. "She likes you, too. I could tell."

Flynn wondered what Killeen based that deduction on. "I'm glad to hear that. I'm taking her to dinner tonight."

"Great. It's high time you dated a woman who's real."

"I draw the line at dating extraterrestrials-in-disguise," Flynn said mildly.

"You could have fooled me," Killeen muttered.

"What?"

"Nothing."

Flynn regarded her. "Insubordination in secretaries is not a trait conducive to a large Christmas bonus."

"When it gets a little closer to Christmas, I'll remember that," Killeen returned.

Flynn withdrew to his office. He'd be in limbo until seven that night anyway. He might as well try and get some work done.

All he could think of was Pride Donovan. Her green eyes were as clear and honest as he remembered, despite what he knew about her duplicity. She had overlaid her former warmth and interest in all his doings with an attitude of gentle mockery.

Her figure was as stunning as ever. Flynn recalled the tiny waist, the long, slender legs, and the high, firm breasts. She had disguised them beneath the business-like blue suit she'd worn, but a discerning male could still spot the attributes.

His body had reacted the instant she walked into his office in that slow, graceful way she had. Even her perfume smelled the same. Pride had always favored a wild rose scent. It recalled their lovemaking to his mind instantly.

Flynn shoved his hands in his pockets and paced the office. Perhaps her story might have been more believable if she hadn't sprung it on him the moment he returned from spending several weeks in Europe on business. The moment he got home, eager to see Pride again, she informed him of her pregnancy.

Pride Donovan had lied to him. She had topped off her lies by following him around for two weeks, demanding that he listen to her. It had been damned embarrassing. He'd better remember that, and quit dwelling on the green eyes and the lovely face with its sculpted planes. Otherwise, he was likely to find himself right back in the same situation.

Flynn sighed. That might not be so bad, come to think about it. Only, this time he'd take damned good care to see that Pride didn't have time to even look at another man.

That trip to Europe had been really bad timing.

*

"I can't believe I'm seeing this," Gloria said.

"You can't believe anything else that's happened today," Pride observed. "Why should this be any different?"

Gloria had marveled all day about Flynn Sutherland's inability to recognize Johnny for what he was.

"If I hadn't witnessed it with my own eyes, I wouldn't have believed it," Gloria said. "Johnny even looks like him." She leaned forward to peer at her cousin's face in the dresser mirror. "Add another one on this side. They look lopsided."

"Freckles always look unbalanced. That's the beauty of them." Pride dotted at her nose with a brown eyebrow pencil. "If Flynn wants to see freckles, here are lots of them to admire."

"You're crazy," Gloria said, with conviction.

"Not me. I always aim to please my man." Pride added a few more dots to her cheekbones with the eyebrow pencil and studied the effect. "Is that natural, or what?"

"Or what," Gloria said.

"Oopsie." Pride grinned at her own nose in the mirror. "Maybe I've gone just a tad overboard. Oh, well. It's too late to do anything about it now. Flynn can consider it revenge for making my nose smell like coffee this morning."

"What are you wearing?"

"An old favorite of Flynn's. Daddy still had all my old clothes carefully preserved in the closet."

Pride rose, fished around in the closet, and withdrew a blue-green silk dress covered with a plastic bag. Flynn had claimed to dislike the dress on the grounds that it made her eyes look blue rather than his favorite green.

"If Flynn wants to see the Pride of three years ago, then that's what he'll see." Pride hoped Flynn suffered a little harmless annoyance over her antics.

"Don't you think you ought to tell him about Johnny?"

"Come on, Gloria." Pride unzipped the plastic bag and took

out the dress. "Would you make things easy for him? You're just sore because you had to pay for lunch."

Gloria grinned back, but her voice was serious. "It's obvious that everything you said about Flynn's single-mindedness is true. It just seems so unfair that his own blindness might rob him of something he'd probably give his right arm for."

"He'll get over it." Pride shored up her mental defenses with all her might in order to show him she was no longer the starry-eyed girl who had loved him so much.

"You don't mean that." Gloria studied her closely. "If you want to know what I think, you're just mad at him."

"You've got that right." She shook out the dress and dropped it over her head. "This time, he's going to have to come to a realization on his own. I'm through beating my head against the wall trying to talk to him. All that ended three years ago."

"Pride, don't let your father's sins wreck your life."

"No one is going to wreck my life," Pride said, with determination. "Or my son's life. So long as Flynn is the slightest bit unsure about who Johnny's father is, he will get no rights to Johnny."

On that, she refused to budge. Her son deserved a father who loved and wanted him. She intended to keep him very far away from Flynn if Flynn so much as hinted at even a tiny little doubt.

She turned her back to let Gloria raise the zipper of the blue-green silk dress and stared at herself in the mirror. Yes, she looked a lot like the Pride Donovan Flynn remembered, and if she tried very hard, she could discuss something other than baby and child care.

The silk dress accentuated her small waist, and the shimmering blue-green color made her eyes look like blue jewels. The only difference between her and the old Pride Donovan was the mass of tawny curls that fell over her shoulders. In Pride's opinion, the new hair color was a definite improvement.

Dinner with Flynn Sutherland. Pride smiled at her freckled self in the mirror and wondered what had gotten into her. More to the point, what had gotten into Flynn? He had made it very clear just what he thought of her and her morals three years ago.

"You're gorgeous, freckles and all," Gloria said. "You'll knock old Flynn's socks off."

"Great. He can eat his heart out." Pride picked up a tiny, leather clutch, checked its contents, and tucked it beneath her arm. "I'd better go kiss Johnny goodnight, or we'll have a little boy trying to follow us out the door."

Johnny and Sylvia had already been tucked into the bed in Pride's old bedroom. Johnny was wide awake when Pride entered. He sat up.

"Johnny Donovan, you're supposed to be asleep," Pride said. "Get back under those covers. You aren't going anywhere."

Johnny pleaded, adding tears when his mother remained adamant.

"No, sir. You've had a busy day today, what with eating Flynn's watch. You need some sleep so your digestive system can get to work on that watch stem."

Johnny retired beneath the covers, sniffing pitifully.

"That's better." Pride leaned down to kiss her son. "Go to sleep, sweetheart. I'll see you in the morning."

She walked into the living room, where Eric and Tracy played with plastic trucks. It had changed little since the day she had last walked out three years before. The heavy green velour carpet was accentuated by the white brocade sofa and padded chairs. Nothing had happened to the pristine furniture yet, but Pride didn't hold out much hope for it, what with four active youngsters in the house.

"I feel awful, letting them play in here." Gloria gestured at the white furniture.

"I hope they wreck it." Pride grimaced. "I used to be afraid to even sit in here."

The doorbell sounded. Pride, conscious of an acceleration of her heartbeat, hastened to open it.

Flynn stared at her. "You look beautiful."

"Thank you." She smiled at him in the manner of one old friend acknowledging another. "So do you."

His white-streaked, dark blond hair had been tamed to sweep across his tanned forehead, and his brown eyes beneath the level brows were dark with unidentifiable emotion. He held out a hand to take hers.

"Flynn's."

Pride whirled. Johnny approached at a run, having shed his pajama bottoms somewhere along the way. He had spotted the watch on Flynn's wrist and wanted to re-stake his claim.

"Oh, no, you don't." She scooped him up. "You're supposed to be in bed, young man. What did you do with your pajamas? Shame on you. Sorry, Flynn. I'll be back with you in a moment."

"Flynn's," Johnny pleaded, stretching his arms toward Flynn.

"That's about the size of it," Pride said. "It's Flynn's, not yours, and you can't have it. It's bedtime."

Johnny fought but was overruled. He filed motion after motion for a review of his case, but his clever tactics only won him a promise of corporal punishment.

He quieted, but his sharp brain remained on the search for mitigating circumstances that would win him a reprieve.

"Flynn's," he said, in insistent tones.

Pride, who sat on the edge of the bed, glanced over her shoulder. Flynn stood in the doorway, watching her.

"That's right. It's Flynn's, not yours. You've done enough damage for one day. Go to sleep."

"Flynn's," Johnny promised.

When Pride tucked the covers beneath his small chin, his large, brown eyes remained fixed on Flynn's left wrist, where the gleam of gold had last been seen.

"I'll see to him," Gloria said. "You'd better go ahead, Pride. This could go on half the night."

"It had better not," Pride said, with a glance at her son that guaranteed dire consequences if it should.

Flynn smiled at Gloria. "He's very active, isn't he? How do you keep up with four of them?"

Gloria looked helplessly at Pride, who had to suppress a chuckle.

"It isn't easy," Pride said. "But it helps if two of them are already in bed. Let's go, Flynn. You're part of the reason Johnny is being such a pain tonight."

Flynn looked back at Johnny and raised a hand in salute. "That kid reminds me of me. I never wanted to go to bed, either."

"Johnny is a real chip off the old block," Pride said. "See you later, Gloria. Call me if there's any trouble."

"Sure," Gloria said, in faint, choked tones. "Have a good time."

Pride walked out the front door and down the sidewalk with Flynn at her side and debated whether to laugh or to cry. Most men would have realized the truth without her having to say a word, but Flynn truly believed he could never father a child.

It was probably for the best, she decided, waiting while Flynn unlocked the door of a dark green Bronco. She'd never allow anyone to make Johnny feel unwanted or unworthy.

Unless Flynn was willing to tell the world that Johnny was his son and he was proud to claim him, she'd see to it that he never got close enough to hurt the little boy.

Never mind that her heart urged her to grab Flynn and shake him until he saw the light. She had to think about Johnny.

"I see your freckles have come back," Flynn noted, handing her into the four-wheel-drive vehicle.

"I knew you'd appreciate the thought."

Flynn studied her in the orange light cast by the setting sun. "You're right. I do. I really missed those freckles today."

He shut the door and came around to slide in beside her. "I thought I'd take you to a place in Houston. It's quiet enough that we can talk business."

"It sounds wonderful. Once I get Daddy's affairs settled, I intend to put the house up for sale."

"You don't want to move back to Anahuac?"

And live where bad memories assaulted her every day? "No, thank you."

The calm, decisive way she spoke seemed to disturb him. He guided the Bronco through the tree-lined streets of the small town toward the highway and contemplated it.

"What are you doing now?" he asked, at last.

"Actually, I'm still into journalism," Pride answered. "I do a lot of the same kind of freelance work."

Pride had worked for various companies as a freelance writer when she lived in Houston. She wrote company histories and contributed regularly to Houston's major newspapers and several regional magazines.

"It came as a shock to me, when I learned you'd been as close as Lake Charles all this time," Flynn said.

He sounded as though he had more to add, but Pride knew better than to get into the details of what she'd been doing.

"What about you, Flynn? When did you open your own office?"

He gave her a wry smile. "I got fed up with taking orders from Dad, if you want to know. I decided to practice general law and still do some work for Dad on the side."

She smiled back, remembering Morgan Sutherland. Morgan had a tendency to run things, including your life, if you let him. When she claimed pregnancy, Morgan had wanted to run one-thousand tests designed to ferret out the truth about her baby's paternity. He also wanted to move Pride in with him and his wife so he could be sure she was well-cared for.

Pride wondered momentarily what Morgan would say if he met Johnny. She smiled. Morgan would probably claim the child right away, regardless of what Flynn said. Morgan was that kind of man.

That was beside the fact that Morgan and Bettricia Sutherland loved children, and Flynn was their only child. They'd had no hope of grandchildren... or so they thought.

"What are you smiling about?" Flynn studied her as well as he could while driving.

Pride decided to forget showing Morgan Sutherland her son. It was Flynn's place to tell his parents about their grandchild.

"I was remembering the way you were always fighting with your father over how the company should be run," she said. "Now that you've left, your life must be boring."

"Actually, Dad respects my opinion now that I'm a self-employed consultant. So long as I was a part of the company, I was a yes-man as far as he was concerned."

"Even though you spent very little time saying yes?"

Flynn laughed and agreed. He began telling her about how he finally decided to leave Sutherland Investments and strike out on his own, and Pride enjoyed listening.

Why shouldn't she? she asked inwardly. After this night, she'd probably never see Flynn Sutherland socially again.

Incredibly, Flynn had other ideas.

"I'd like to take you out in the boat tomorrow afternoon," he said. "Do you think Gloria and the children would enjoy it?"

Pride turned her incredulous gaze toward him and wondered what on earth had gotten into Flynn. "Of course they'd enjoy it. The real question is, are you sane?"

He grinned. "Why do you say that?"

"Because you've obviously lost your mind. Have you any idea what it's like to have four children below the age of five together on a boat? Together, period? When did you get so fascinated by children?"

Flynn drove in silence a moment. That silence confirmed her deduction. In the past three years, Flynn had been examining the idea of having children and found it pleasant.

"Since you told me you were pregnant," he said, at last. "Before then, children hadn't entered into my plans. I grew up knowing I couldn't have any of my own, so I put it out of my mind and planned to adopt at some point in the distant future."

"You aren't sterile, Flynn," she said, with extreme patience. "I suspect you have a low sperm count. That is not the same as sterile. Remember the basic premise of human biology. All it takes is one sperm and one egg."

"The doctors all said I was sterile," Flynn said, in the adamant tones that brooked no argument. "Do you think I wanted to believe you had another lover? It nearly killed me."

Pride had run out of patience with this statement. "I'm glad to hear that, because it was pretty devastating to me, too."

"Don't bother lying to me at this late date."

"Well, when you find out his identity, please tell me."

The days for letting him make her angry with that accusation were over. She had long ago forced herself to recognize that if he refused to see the truth, there was no way she was going to make him. She counted to ten, breathed deeply, and dug her nails into her palms until she almost believed herself calm.

"I never found out who he was," Flynn said, in grim tones. "I'll say this for you. You covered your tracks well."

Astonished, Pride turned her head to stare at him a moment. He still sounded absolutely furious. It might have happened yesterday as far as Flynn was concerned.

Somehow, knowing he still felt hurt and angry gave Pride hope. Perhaps he would work his way toward the truth.

On the other hand, she reminded herself, the truth might make no difference to Flynn. She had no business hoping Flynn would love her again.

She drew in a deep breath. "While you're working on the problem of my secret lover, see another doctor. It sounds to me like your old one was so interested in preparing you for the worst he forgot to mention the possibility of miracles."

"I've lost interest, thank you," Flynn said.

She fell silent, staring out the side window at the tall marsh grass that covered the coastal plains. Three years ago, she'd worn herself into a nervous breakdown trying to prove herself to Flynn, and look where it had gotten her. He still thought her a liar.

"I didn't mean to hash over the past," he said, at last. "I promised myself I'd forget it, at least for tonight. Will you forgive me and let's start over again?"

Flynn laying on the charm was worse than Flynn raising hell. She responded too much. Pride kept her face turned to the window while she struggled to get her unruly emotions under control.

"Of course. Shall we discuss taking the kids out on your boat? You're asking for trouble, you know."

Flynn laughed. "With three adults, we ought to be able to handle four children, don't you think?"

"Not if Johnny keeps lusting after your watch."

"I'm developing a deep liking for Johnny. He's a boy after my own heart," Flynn said, and rendered his companion speechless.

Pride found her voice at last. "He seems to have taken to you, too. He's the most stubborn child I've ever dealt with."

Of all the exquisite ironies, that Flynn enjoyed Johnny's company and didn't realize the boy was his son.

"You know what they say about birds of a feather," Flynn pointed out. "We stick together."

And how. "When he eats the rest of your watch, don't complain to me about its sentimental value."

She ought to tell him now. But Flynn was not yet ready to believe her. She held her breath until the urge passed.

"Johnny and I are forming a mutual admiration society," Flynn went on.

Speechless, Pride keep her face composed and her gaze straight ahead while she imagined Flynn's feelings if he ever realized on his own that Johnny was his son.

She grinned suddenly. Perhaps she could suggest that Flynn offer to adopt the child from Gloria on the grounds that Gloria had too many children already. She could just picture Gloria's indignant refutation of Flynn's offer.

What would be even funnier was Flynn's face when Gloria told him that Johnny, the child after his own heart, was Pride's son rather than Gloria's.

Chapter Three

Flynn felt vaguely disturbed long before he drove beneath the blue awning that sheltered the entrance to the restaurant he had chosen. Pride's refusal to argue with him any further over her baby's parentage hadn't escaped him, nor had the fleeting expression of private amusement on her face.

Neither had those ridiculous freckles she'd dabbed on her cheeks, or the blue-green dress he remembered disliking.

He considered the matter as he drove. He'd far rather have Pride screaming at him, the way she had three years ago. It would have meant she still cared, that she was still wanted to convince him that yes, she had been pregnant, and no, she hadn't taken another lover.

The Pride who sat quietly beside him, however, stated her position plainly and shut up. She made it clear that she didn't care any longer what he believed or whether he found her attractive.

Flynn pondered it with a sense of insulted disquiet and watched her surreptitiously. For the most part, she sat with her hands folded in her lap, the picture of tranquility. At times a smile broke across her face like rays of sunshine, and he wondered who brought that tender look to her face.

Astonished, he realized that he couldn't stand it. "Pride?"

She looked at him as if her thoughts had been more interesting than his company.

"What are you thinking?"

Three years ago, he could ask her that question and receive an answer that would send the blood singing through his veins.

She smiled. "I was thinking about Johnny. If you take him on your boat, you'll have to tie him to the mast. Otherwise, he's sure to fall into the water."

"Like that time you wound up in the water?"

"I got caught by the wind," Pride said, with dignity. "You'd better plan some way to keep the children confined to the deck if you really intend to take them sailing."

"I'll think of something," he promised.

Why was Pride thinking about Johnny? Probably, she was covering up her thoughts of a new boyfriend in Lake Charles.

He hated to ask, but he couldn't stand not knowing.

"Are you dating anyone special?" He cursed himself because the question didn't sound nearly as casual as he hoped.

"No."

He'd have sworn Pride told the absolute truth, but he'd been fooled by Pride before. He'd better remember that, and rip out this growing desire to believe anything she told him, or she would really rake his heart over the fire this time.

"Why not?" he asked.

"Are you?" she countered.

"No, because I've been too busy establishing my practice to put a lot of time into developing a so-called meaningful relationship," he said and smiled at her astonished expression.

"Good for you." She sounded half-choked.

"Well?"

"Well, what?"

"Why aren't you dating anyone special?"

"Like you, I've been too busy making a living to cultivate interpersonal connections."

Flynn began to laugh. He'd forgotten how entertaining it was to hear the way Pride phrased things.

"Don't you remember?" he asked. "In my office this morning, I told you that you're now a relatively rich woman. You don't have to work any more if you don't want to."

"Is that right?"

She really thought he was lying. Flynn's eyes widened with shock. "When I show you your father's stock portfolio, you'll understand."

"I didn't know he had one," Pride said. "How interesting."

Her tone implied it was anything but. Flynn considered that a moment, recalling what she'd said earlier about her father. "Is it true your father believed you weren't his daughter?"

"Heavens, Flynn, do you think I'd say so if it weren't? Yes, it was true, and yes, you can probably check it out if you're sufficiently interested. He used it as an excuse to be rude to Mama in public constantly. It was almost a relief to me when she died, because she'd never have to put up with that again."

It was the longest speech Pride had ever made about her childhood. Flynn had never thought of it before, but he knew almost nothing about Pride's upbringing. That was strange, because Judge Alan Donovan had been a fixture at the courthouse in Anahuac for as long as Flynn could remember. He was known as a tough, but fair, judge.

Puzzled, Flynn glanced at her. "Why didn't you tell me any of this when we were dating?"

"Why should I? It had nothing to do with you, and there's nothing more boring than having to listen to the more horrid parts of someone else's childhood."

Flynn spotted the restaurant and guided the Bronco beneath the blue canopy that marked the entrance. "I would have been interested."

"I'm sure you would," Pride said, in that same flat tones she used when she refused to argue with him about her pregnancy.

Flynn found it a stunning shock to realize that she had no intention of arguing with him about his interest in her childhood any more than she intended to argue with him about her alleged baby's father. Her attitude said something to him, and it took Flynn a moment to get a grasp on what it was.

He sat still a moment, ignoring the restaurant employee who intended to park his car.

Years ago he had watched his college roommate suffer through a love affair that was on and off so many times, that at last all the feeling had been burned out of the man. When the woman came back one last time, Flynn's roommate wore that same patient, detached expression he saw now on Pride's face.

She no longer cared. She didn't care anymore about her father and had long ago given up on ever winning his love.

And she no longer cared about Flynn Sutherland, or about convincing him that he had gotten her pregnant.

"Flynn? That man is waiting," Pride said.

Flynn stared at her and wondered if he were seeing her for the first time. How had he missed the distant attitude she projected, or the aloof expression in her green eyes?

He felt as if he'd stepped down and discovered too late that there was no step where he expected one to be.

He got out hastily and came around to open her door and help her down. Her hand felt soft and cool, and it didn't linger in his one second longer than necessary.

Flynn hated it.

Perhaps it was a judgment on him. He'd spent so much time telling himself Pride was trying to trick him into marriage, he had never considered that she might just lose interest.

He placed his hand at her back in the old way and walked her into the restaurant. Sure enough, Pride moved slightly away, so slightly he wouldn't have noticed if he hadn't been expecting it. When he took her arm to escort her to their table, she behaved as if she was unsure of his name.

Flynn seated her, conscious of an unreasoning desire to jerk her into his arms and force her to care again. One couldn't behave like a Neanderthal in public, so he pushed the desire aside and sat down across from her. She took up the menu, glanced at it without much interest, and laid it back down.

"Please order for me," she said. "I still like all the same things."

Except him. Flynn wondered at his own blindness. He'd noted her wariness earlier in his office, but he hadn't recognized her cousin and the four children as a deliberate distancing tool.

Pride looked around the restaurant in a pleased way. A few moments ago, Flynn would have cynically assumed it was because he had chosen an expensive French restaurant. Now he realized she thought he wouldn't get too personal in a place like this.

"This must be a popular place to eat." Pride maneuvered her chair to change her position a bit.

Flynn glanced up and discovered the reason. His parents had a table nearby, and Pride now had her back more fully to them.

"The food and the service are both first class," Flynn said. "That's why I brought you here."

Three years ago, Pride had been thankful to dine with him at the nearest pizza parlor. She enjoyed everything they did together. That effervescent joy in his presence had been one of the most powerfully attractive things about her.

He studied her, debating the best approach to breaking down her reserve. Her eyes, a mysterious blue-green thanks to her dress and the low lighting, held a watchful expression.

She behaved almost the way he had behaved three years ago, Flynn suddenly realized, when he regarded everything she said as a lie. It was an unpleasant sensation to find the tables turned.

"Good evening, Flynn. May I present myself to your—Why, Pride Donovan. I almost didn't recognize you."

Flynn's father, a tall man with greying brown hair and brown eyes like Flynn's stood beside them and regarded Pride with an expression somewhere between surprise and pleasure. Morgan Sutherland had always claimed Pride was the sort of woman he hoped Flynn would marry.

Flynn noted Pride's expression automatically. Although her

mouth smiled, she regarded Morgan Sutherland in much the same way she had been regarding him. In fact, Flynn thought there might be more warmth in Pride's gaze as she faced his father.

"My dear, I should have realized you'd be in town," Morgan said. "I'm so sorry about your father's passing."

Pride smiled and said, "Thank you. You're very kind."

"My wife and I would like the opportunity to visit with you further while you're here. Will you stop by our apartment later for coffee?"

"Thank you, but I left my cousin at home with four small children. I don't want to leave her alone any longer than absolutely necessary."

Morgan Sutherland was unaccustomed to refusals. "Perhaps tomorrow night. You can bring your cousin and the children. It's been too long since we've had children in the house."

"If you're wise, you'll make it a while longer," Pride said, still smiling. "Placing four small children together in one place is asking for mayhem of the worst kind."

"It sounds wonderful," Morgan said, satisfied. "Tomorrow night. It's settled. Bettricia will be thrilled."

Pride wasn't. That much was obvious to Flynn.

"I'm afraid it won't be possible," she said, "but thank you all the same."

Morgan immediately began to present ways and means by which it was possible, and Pride just as adroitly evaded them.

"I don't think you want to have coffee with us," Morgan said, balked.

Pride, still smiling said, "No, sir. I don't."

Morgan stared.

"That's honest enough for you, Dad," Flynn said, laughing at his father's astounded expression.

"If that's so, then I'm sorry," Morgan said. "I had hoped we could forget the past and make a fresh start. Bettricia and I always thought very highly of you, until you claimed Flynn as the father of your child."

"That's really very kind of you," Pride said. "As I recall, I made quite an uproar."

"You did," Morgan said grimly. "It was damned embarrassing. What on earth got into you, young lady?"

Pride's face took on a set look of remembered suffering. "At the time, it seemed the only thing I could do."

"Dad." Flynn stared at Pride, once more conscious of something he couldn't yet define. "Leave it alone, please."

Morgan Sutherland had been ignoring his son's advice for years. Flynn wasn't surprised when he continued to do so.

"Flynn told us he had informed you long before you claimed you were pregnant that he couldn't possibly father a child," Morgan said. "Whatever possessed you to claim that he had? Surely you realized we'd all know you were lying."

Pride's sudden smile lit her face in the old way. "Did it ever occur to you that I thought Flynn had been lying to me? He told me he couldn't get me pregnant, and he did. How do you think I felt when that happened?"

There was an appalled silence. Flynn felt as if he had been turned to stone.

Morgan said at last, "I'm terribly sorry, Pride. There isn't much we can say to you, is there?"

*

Pride watched Morgan Sutherland march back to his table with a combined sense of regret and relief. She loved the older man and his wife, but she could not imagine spending several hours trying to pretend she was the girl they remembered, all in the presence of her little boy.

Besides, for all she knew, Morgan and Bettricia Sutherland

might well take one look at Johnny and realize the truth.

Not that it would make any difference to Flynn. He might well deny the possibility that Johnny was his child.

Flynn stared at her as if he had just noticed her. Pride met his eyes briefly then looked away and watched the waiter set out water and offer Flynn the wine list.

Flynn started and took the list, swiftly placing orders for both wine and food. The moment the waiter left, he leaned forward. "Did you really think I lied to you?"

"The thought crossed my mind." She faced him and told him the absolute truth. "Come on, Flynn. What would you think if a woman told you she couldn't get pregnant because she was on the pill, then she said she was pregnant?"

Flynn sat in appalled silence a moment.

"I see," he said, at last. "So you thought I was taking advantage of your innocence just so I could get you into bed with me?"

Pride smiled. "Yes, I did think that for a while. Then I realized you really believed in that sterile bit, so I had to acquit you of being out to seduce me."

"What did you think when I refused to listen to you?"

Pride glanced at him. He sounded calm and reasonable, unlike the way he usually reacted when this subject came up.

"I didn't know what to think at first. It shocked me to realize you actually wanted to believe I had another lover."

Flynn's expression didn't change, but he looked bleak suddenly. "You thought I wanted to believe you were running around on me?"

"What else could I think? If you had been halfway interested in proving I was a liar, you'd have had those medical tests redone by another doctor." She reached for her wine glass, needing fortification badly. "Let's discuss about something else, Flynn. I'm through talking about this."

"My parents had those tests repeated several times when I was a teenager. Dad was more interested than I was in my future ability to have children. I couldn't see repeating them yet again." He paused, staring at her. "It wasn't exactly fun to keep dwelling on my personal failings."

Pride leaned back in her chair. "I wouldn't call it a personal failing. As far as I'm concerned, you were potent and virile and all those other words denoting masculine achievement in fathering a child."

After a moment of stunned silence, Flynn burst into laughter. The pinched, gray look left his face, and warmth blazed from the penny-brown eyes. He reached across the table, holding his hand palm-up.

"You always know the perfect thing to say to a man, don't you? Give me your hand, sweetheart."

"What for?" Pride held onto her prickly attitude with both hands. Now was not the time to let Flynn into her heart again.

"Because I want to hold it."

"Oh, yes?" She eyed his hand a moment. "You aren't going to kiss it or anything revolting like that, are you?"

"I just want to hold it a minute."

She glanced at her gold watch. "One minute then."

Flynn laughed and closed his fingers over the slim hand that settled into his. Then he met her eyes. "I don't quite know how to say this, Pride."

"Then perhaps you'd better not. Thirty seconds."

"Your watch is fast. Look, Pride, I—"

"Oh, thank you, Flynn. I haven't eaten shrimp cocktail in ages."

The waiter returned with appetizers, and Pride withdrew her hand when Flynn's grip loosened. She picked up her fork and ignored his outstretched hand.

"Pride, I'm trying to say something to you. Would you mind paying attention for a minute here?"

"Save it for later," Pride recommended. "I'm busy. I really appreciate this. I do love a good shrimp cocktail."

"You've never been a chatterer," Flynn observed. "What is it you're afraid I'm going to say to you?"

Pride popped a large shrimp dipped in red cocktail sauce into her mouth. She had to finish it off before she could reply to his question. The task kept her from splashing the contents of her wine glass in his face.

"I have no idea," she said, at last. "But I'll tell you this. If you're about to state that now, after all I went through three years ago, you have suddenly achieved a belief in my innate honesty such that you now accept my assertions that you are the father of my child, I'll dump this entire dish of shrimp cocktail over your head." She dipped another shrimp in the sauce and waved it at him. "It would be a sad waste of good shrimp."

"Is that so?" Flynn withdrew his outstretched hand. "How about if I say I now have an open mind on the subject?"

Pride chewed another shrimp in a thoughtful way. "I'd say you always had an open mind. Everything I said went in one ear and out the other."

"Now who has the open mind?" Flynn asked.

She grinned across the table cheerfully. "An open mind is the chief characteristic of a good journalist."

"You aren't going to listen to me, are you?"

"Well, it wouldn't be fair, would it?"

"What do you mean?"

"I mean far be it from me to deprive you of the opportunity to follow me around for two weeks or so, screaming at me in public and interrupting my dates with other men."

When he said nothing, she gave him a brilliant smile. "I'm a very fair person," she finished.

"Yes, I can see you are." Flynn picked up his own fork. "I suppose I have no right to complain about that."

"You can't think how glad I am to hear you say so." Pride made a great effort and managed not to throw her napkin at him. "All right, Flynn. I'm here tonight because you're supposed to explain to me, in terms I can understand, all about the multi-million-dollar inheritance I'm about to come into."

"Did I say multi-million? It's more like two-million."

"Come on, Flynn. Daddy was too busy judging people to play the stock market, or whatever he did to make all this money."

"He invested in the stock market," Flynn said. "Quite well, as it happens. You own a lot of stock in growth industries, like computer companies and trash-removal companies."

"Trash removal companies?"

"It may be inelegant, but you have to admit, it's a growth industry." Flynn paused and regarded her over his wine glass. "There will be taxes, of course, but you'll receive a tidy estate once I've finished all the paper work." He smiled. "Are you really going to Bermuda?"

"Actually, it was a joke. Gloria and I laughed all the way to Anahuac about what we were going to do with the penny Daddy left me."

"I think he was depending on me to make you understand that he wanted to apologize for the past." Flynn studied her. "I'm sorry, Pride. If I had been able to get to the hospital right away, I might have been able to find out what he wanted to say."

"There's no need to feel sorry." Pride found herself unable to think about her father just then. "If Daddy had wanted to make amends, he could have written me a letter anytime."

"Did he know where you were?"

"It wouldn't have taken much work for him to find out."

Flynn looked annoyed, as if he didn't believe her when she pointed out that her whereabouts shouldn't have been difficult for Alan Donovan to discover.

"He was probably afraid to face me," she said.

"Why?"

She hesitated, while she expunged from her mind the fact that Alan Donovan knew she hadn't miscarried. "Perhaps he was afraid of admitting, even to himself, that I was his daughter. Especially after I went off and got myself into trouble."

Flynn winced. "No one makes a big deal out of unwed motherhood these days."

"Except self-righteous men like my father."

Flynn wisely changed the subject. "You'll be able to afford to pick and choose your freelance assignments now. Maybe you can even start the great American novel."

"I've never had any aspirations as a novelist. I'm more of a nonfiction type." She looked at her empty cocktail dish thoughtfully. "Actually, I do have an idea in mind for a book."

"I'd like to see you write a book," Flynn said. "What will it be about?"

"I'll have to think on it a bit more before I go telling people about it." She was not about to tell Flynn about the book outline she had already completed. "Did you tell everyone ahead of time that you were about to quit your dad's firm and strike out on your own?"

"No." Flynn smiled wryly. "Everyone was aware of it all the same. You could hear Dad shouting for three blocks."

"He seems resigned to your absence now," she commented.

"Even he recognized the force of my arguments when I pointed out that I wasn't particularly useful to the firm in my position as his understudy. He was going out of his way to keep me from doing any actual work."

"I remember," she murmured.

Flynn had been trained in business and law in preparation for taking over Sutherland Investments one day, but when he went to work for the firm, Morgan discovered he was nowhere near wanting to give up any of his power to his son. Privately, she thought Flynn had been wise to leave the company for a while.

"I suppose you would remember," Flynn said, in dry tones. "We get along much better now." He paused and studied her face. "Are you holding a grudge against my parents?"

"Heavens, no. You heard your father. He likes me."

"They mourned your departure for weeks," Flynn said, to her surprise. "Dad was of the opinion that I should have married you and treated the baby as my own."

"On the grounds that you aren't able to have a child of your own and adoption is ridiculously difficult?" Pride managed a smile and gripped her hands together in her lap. "Now that's an idea. Gee, why didn't I think to suggest that?"

Flynn started to say something, but apparently thought better of it when he caught her gaze.

Their waiter arrived with food, and Pride breathed a sigh of relief. Flynn had ordered her a steak marinated in a French herb sauce. Too bad she had totally lost her appetite for the succulent dish. Worse, Flynn kept staring at her every time he thought her attention was focused on the food.

When their plates were removed at long last and cups of steaming coffee were set before them, Pride curled her fingers around her cup and let herself relax a little. Surely, the evening was almost over.

"You still haven't explained about my inheritance," she pointed out. "We seem to keep getting off the subject."

Flynn smiled. "I've told you, but you don't seem to believe me. Why don't you come to the office in the morning and I'll show you some of the paperwork, and what you can expect in terms of income."

Pride thought about it. Maybe she'd better go and get it over with. "All right. What time?"

"Eleven. Prepare to have lunch with me. I want to show you a new boat I'm thinking about buying, then we'll take Gloria and the kids sailing."

Pride stared at her cup, dismayed at the fierce longing that arose inside her. "I don't know about this, Flynn."

"Gloria and the kids will enjoy the outing. This is a family boat we're going to see."

"Oh, yes? Is there such a thing?"

"Of course. If the children don't fall overboard, I'll buy the boat. How's that?"

"I'd call it a good test," Pride agreed.

She wanted to go, she realized, astonished at herself. She longed to see the marina again. She'd thought Flynn was kidding, when he claimed he'd take everyone out on his boat.

Johnny would love it, which was, of course, the only reason she even considered it.

Flynn smiled. "Then I'll expect you tomorrow morning at eleven. You and I will need to spend about half an hour together then we'll pack up the children and drive to Galveston. You're going to love this boat."

"I'm sure I will." The only things Pride knew about boats were the things Flynn had taught her.

"I've been thinking about a motor yacht," Flynn said.

"You? A motor yacht? A stinker? A noisemaker?"

"I've been... considering something that would be comfortable for a family," Flynn said slowly. "My old sailboat is too small, and it definitely isn't a family-type boat."

"A family," Pride repeated. Was Flynn thinking about marriage and adoption? "Well, I'll tell you what, Flynn. When Johnny gets aboard, you'll have a very good test of its child-worthiness. He's in an exploring stage right now."

"Great," Flynn said. "I'll count on Johnny. Are you ready? I want to show you another place I discovered recently."

"I'd rather go home, if you don't mind. As I told your dad, it wasn't fair of me to leave Gloria alone with the kids."

"It won't take but a minute." He stood and helped her rise. "You'll enjoy it. Would you mind speaking to my mother before we leave?"

Pride couldn't think of a good reason for avoiding Flynn's mother, much as she'd have liked to. She allowed Flynn to lead her to his parents' table and tried to steel herself.

"Pride, dear, thank you for stopping to speak," Bettricia Sutherland said, in almost humble tones. "You haven't changed."

Bettricia was an elegant, faded blonde, with a slender figure and soft, blue eyes. She was a tender-hearted woman who lived for her husband and her son.

Pride, conscious of the dotted-on freckles on her nose, clasped the older woman's hand warmly. "Neither have you. It's so nice to see the two of you again, and to visit Houston again."

"You were never full of platitudes before," Morgan Sutherland observed. "In fact, we liked you because you were so warm and genuine. Have we injured you that deeply by our actions three years ago?"

"Dad, can't you leave the subject alone? Surely you can see Pride doesn't care for it."

"I'm not hurt at all," Pride said, at once. "If you want to know the truth, I was surprised you spoke to me tonight. I caused you both a lot of trouble and heartache."

"That's true enough." Morgan's gaze went over her slightly too slender figure. "The question is, how much did you suffer? Has Flynn even bothered to find out?"

"Dad—"

The situation had almost progressed beyond saving, Pride saw. Morgan had decided he was responsible in some way for her well-being, and he wouldn't hesitate to try and take her over.

"There was never anything wrong with me," Pride said quietly. "Flynn has nothing to find out about, or to reproach himself about."

Morgan's brown gaze, so like Flynn's, never moved from her face. He said nothing, but the determined expression on his face told her clearly that he wasn't done with the subject.

"It's nice to see you both again," Pride said. "If you'll excuse us, I need to get home to my cousin."

She nodded pleasantly, trying not to notice the tears that had filled Bettricia's soft, blue eyes, and turned away in obedience to the gentle pressure of Flynn's hand at her back.

"I'm sorry about Dad's refusal to stay off the forbidden subject," Flynn said as they walked toward the door. "He worried about you after you left."

"Did he?"

"Yes, he did." He added, "So did I."

Chapter Four

Pride gave him a dazzling smile. "There was no need for anyone to worry about me. As you can see, I'm flourishing."

"Yes, I see that," Flynn said, "although your freckles don't look quite the same as the sun-kissed variety."

"Now, Flynn, if you want freckles, you'll get freckles. I thought I did a good job."

"You did, except for this big one on the left side of your nose. It looks a bit unbalanced."

"Too bad," Pride leaped on the change of subject. "My hand must have faltered at a critical moment."

"I think I can help out in this situation," Flynn said.

Before she could protest, Flynn wrapped his arms around her, and his lips descended on the side of her nose. For a brief instant, she shoved hard at him, but she was no match for his strength. She stood passively while he caressed the offending dot with his tongue then reached up to rub at her nose with his finger tip.

"Too bad" he said. "Looks like I've damaged a few of the others."

"I feel a lawsuit coming on," she began, and Flynn's warm mouth covered hers.

Astounded, Pride closed her eyes to shut out his face while he kissed her with enormous deliberation, as if they stood in the privacy of his apartment rather than the busy foyer of a restaurant.

"Your car is here, sir," the doorman said, when Flynn lifted his head at last.

Flynn smiled into Pride's dazed, green eyes. "Now you look even more unbalanced. I'd better tend to the other side."

Pride recovered herself. "Thank you, I'll tend to it myself."

She fell silent while he helped her into his Bronco. Why was Flynn kissing her? Nothing made any sense. The kiss left her in such a whirl, she hardly knew her own name.

Flynn climbed in, and his thoughtful expression encouraged her to swiftly wet the lace-edged handkerchief in her purse and scrub at the freckles penciled on her nose and cheeks.

"Actually, I was getting used to them," he said.

"Sorry. Maybe I should try getting some sun."

"Tomorrow," he promised. "The weather should be great."

He started the engine and guided the vehicle out of the drive and onto the street.

Pride said nothing, but the tumult inside her fairly shouted out a warning. She still wanted Flynn. She must be crazy. She had to be. Worse, she wanted him to make love to her again. She was clearly, certifiably, indubitably, insane.

But Johnny needed a little brother or sister. Surely that need mitigated her insanity a bit.

"What are you smiling about, Pride?"

"I was wondering how much longer your watch was going to live after further exposure to Johnny. He's a very tenacious little boy, Flynn. Maybe you'd better use your cell phone like everyone else these days."

Flynn laughed and showed her his elegant, gold mariner's watch. She peered at the colorful, nautical flags on the face. So far as she could tell, the watch still kept perfect time.

"I'll have it fixed one of these days."

"Once Johnny eats the face, you'll have to invest in a new watch."

"It'll be worth it."

"Let's hope you still think so, when I send you the bill for the operation to remove various little metal parts from his insides."

"All kids eat peculiar things. My particular experiences along that line are legendary. Just ask Dad."

Pride chuckled. "I might do that."

She'd enjoy knowing of another likeness between Flynn and Johnny, although it looked like she'd never be able to share the likeness with the person most concerned.

Flynn had turned the car into another parking lot and was guiding it into a parking space before Pride realized they had left the street.

"I thought you were taking me home."

"I'm taking you dancing. We won't stay long."

Being around Flynn in a busy restaurant was one thing. Being alone with him on a dance floor was quite another.

"I'd rather not," she said, almost breathless with the desire to dance with him. Just once, she promised herself.

"I know, but we're going anyway." He glanced at her as he released his seat belt. "You can endure dancing with me for twenty or thirty minutes, can't you?"

She feared she'd do far more than endure it. She feared she'd enjoy it outrageously. That was the problem.

He came swiftly around to help her down. "I've changed my mind about that dress."

Startled, she looked up. His penny-brown eyes were warm and merry, which, at the moment, was more seductive to Pride than his most passionate kisses and apologetic speeches would have been.

"You remember it?" she managed. "I'm surprised."

"I've never forgotten anything about you," he said.

Feeling considerably shaken, Pride gave him her hand and stepped down. Obviously, this dancing idea was a bigger mistake than she thought.

She tried to remove her hand from his clasp as soon as her feet were on the pavement, but he refused to let go. Instead, he tucked her hand through his arm in the old way and walked her toward the nightclub. Pride panicked when she noted that her overly responsive senses had detected the warmth of his body as he walked close beside her.

The band played a slow, soft tune when Flynn seated her at a small table near the dance floor. Maybe she should spend the time scarfing down cocktails rather than dancing in Flynn's arms.

She hadn't been seated a minute when Flynn rose and took her hand. "Let's dance."

The music changed to a slow waltz. She went into Flynn's arms, feeling almost as if time had rolled back.

He held her way too close. Pride made a vain attempt to keep her distance, but his arms proved strong and unyielding. Before she knew it, her cheek rested on his chest, and his hand at her back pressed her against his body.

"You move like an angel," he said in her ear.

Pride repressed a tingle of reaction to those words and said only, "Thank you."

Flynn's soft laughter stirred her hair. "Aren't you going to tell me I dance like Fred Astaire?"

She had once responded to his compliments with compliments of her own. "I'll pass judgment on you after a few more dances."

"Good. We'll stay as long as you want to dance," Flynn said.

She wanted to dance with him forever. That realization struck her with shattering effect.

As if he knew her thoughts, Flynn brought her even closer to his body, letting her feel his hard strength and the power of his embrace. Pride gasped and wondered if she could last through another few dances with Flynn Sutherland. Her body already longed to undergo a form of core meltdown.

The band, for once, cooperated with Pride's head, if not her traitorous body. It shifted from the waltz into a snappy rock number.

"Let's sit down," Flynn said. "I want to make a few requests."

He settled her at their table once more, ordered her a glass of wine, and crossed the floor to confer with the band leader. Moments later, she saw him drop money into the kitty.

"What did you request?" she asked, when he returned.

Flynn smiled. "A few things you like."

Pride gulped. Was Flynn trying to resurrect her feelings for him by recreating the things she had once responded to? Perhaps he liked her performance in bed so much, he wanted a repeat.

If so, he certainly knew how to go about it.

The band slid into a slow version of a Beatles tune Pride loved. Flynn reached for her hand at once and led her onto the dance floor.

She could not allow this to happen, she realized belatedly.

"Flynn? Do you still plan on adopting children someday?"

The question startled him. She detected the sudden tension in his arms.

"Perhaps," he said. "Why do you ask?"

"I was just wondering. You aren't really sterile, you know. If you fall in love with the right woman, and conditions are truly compatible, you might just surprise yourself."

His soft laughter tickled her hair, and seconds later, she felt his lips on her temple.

"I hope so," he said. "With adoption the way it is these days, I'll be fifty before I make it to the top of the lists."

Pride fastened on that. "Of course, you could go on a do-it-yourself kick and take out one of those ads in the personal columns. 'Rich attorney and full-time Mom with lovely home, fenced yard, and lots of love seek to adopt your newborn baby.'"

"I haven't even hooked up with that truly compatible woman yet." Flynn cuddled her closer, despite her attempts to look into his face. "What do you suggest I look for?"

Her writer's creative instincts swung into high gear. "The first thing you should do, as soon as you have a likely prospect, is have a compatibility check done."

"Is that so? What the heck is a compatibility check?"

Pride grinned against his chest. "That's where the doctors check out your sperm and her eggs to make sure they won't hate each other upon sight. It seems that there are all kinds of little parts on a woman that can develop fierce, allergic reactions to the complimentary parts on a man." She waited an instant, before adding helpfully, "I believe it's a common cause of infertility."

"Is that so?"

"Yes, indeed. They forgot to get their little parts checked out for compatibility. Instead, they fell in love."

"Terrible," Flynn murmured. "Really terrible."

"If children are the desired result, that's a fact," Pride told him, tongue-in-cheek.

"There ought to be a law."

"You're an attorney. Draft one." She searched her memory for the research she'd once done for an article. "In the meantime, however, there are several techniques available for males with your particular problem."

"Really?"

Knowing Morgan Sutherland, Pride suspected he had already informed Flynn of every option available. "Yes, indeed. For one thing, when a man has a low sperm count, they can actually concentrate the sperm—"

"Pride."

"Yes, Flynn?" She smiled into his shirt.

"Shut up."

"No, Flynn, I don't think I will. Those days are over. It's time you realized I intend to speak when and where I please, on what I please." She lifted her head, with her most challenging smile. "If you don't like it, why don't you just leave me on the dance floor while you turn around and stalk off?"

Flynn smiled back. Oddly enough, he didn't look angry.

"Leaving you to catch a cab back to Anahuac?" he asked.

"Actually, I'd call Gloria to come get me. Once she got here, we'd get a motel room, now that I'm rich, and spend tomorrow shopping wildly at the Galleria."

"You still don't believe you're rich?"

"My suspicious attitude has nothing to do with you being the lawyer to spring it on me," she assured him.

"Thank you." Flynn held her against him. "Your faith in my integrity is most touching."

"I've never doubted your integrity, Flynn," Pride said, in earnest tones. "Your intelligence, yes, but your integrity, no."

There was a beat of silence, then Flynn burst into laughter that had couples near them glancing their way.

"I suppose I'm lucky you've consented to let me hold you like this," he said.

"I don't mind dumb men. It's the dishonest ones I can't stand. You know. The ones who swear up and down they'll take care of you no matter what."

Flynn came to an abrupt halt, causing Pride to stumble over his foot. His lean face suddenly looked hard and set.

"All right," he said. "I suppose I deserved that. Get your purse. I'll take you home."

Pride snatched up her small, leather clutch on the run as Flynn, his hand at her back, hurried her out of the club. He didn't slow down until they arrived at his Bronco.

Rather than unlock the door swiftly to lift her in, he stood staring at her in the semi-darkness, making no move to fish his keys from his pocket.

"It occurred to me recently—" he began.

"Do you mean, tonight?"

"Recently," he went on, ignoring her, "that you have reason to be considerably upset with me, even assuming your baby was fathered by someone else."

Pride caught her breath. He still thought she was lying. He still thought she'd slept with another man.

Gritting her teeth, she said, "I'm not upset with you."

He ignored that. "I did promise to take care of you." He stared at the ground. "When you said you were pregnant, I was so angry, I—forgot all my promises to you." His gaze met hers squarely. "I went back on everything I said. I'm sorry, Pride."

Now that it was too late, Pride wished she had never pushed things to this extreme. "Lots of men promise a woman everything so they can get her into bed."

"Is that what you thought I was doing?"

She managed a shrug. "What do you think?"

Flynn's brown eyes flashed. "I meant everything I said to you." He reached out and grabbed her shoulders so suddenly, she didn't have time to step back out of reach. "I loved you."

"I loved you, and look what it got me."

"What did it get you?" The anger left his face suddenly as his gaze slid over her too-slender figure and locked on her face. "I'd really like to know."

He produced his keys and unlocked the car door, then helped her step inside. Stunned, Pride buckled on her seat belt while her gaze followed Flynn as he walked around to slide in beside her.

"What do you mean?" she asked.

"I'd like you to tell me everything that happened after you closed out your Houston apartment and left the area for good."

Pride shook her head numbly. Did that mean he wanted to hear all about her alleged miscarriage?

"I'll do that, if you can answer one question for me."

Flynn sat silently, staring out the windshield and making no move to start the engine.

"Do you still believe my baby wasn't yours?"

"Dammit, Pride, look at it from my point of view," he exploded. "You claim that one unprotected incident resulted in your pregnancy, and you totally ignore the fact that, even if I have a very low sperm count rather than total sterility, it would still require a lot of luck and a lot of effort before I could get a woman pregnant."

"You forgot the compatibility check." Pride grappled with a sudden desire to bop him with her purse. "You also forgot that all it takes to make a baby is contact between one sperm and one egg. Sorry, Flynn. I don't feel the need or the desire to tell you what happened after I left. I'm surprised you'd even want to hear it."

She clenched her fists in her lap as Flynn started the car with an air of suppressed violence. After all the time she'd spent ridding herself of the anger and despair she'd felt at Flynn's refusal to accept the truth, Pride was astounded to find herself literally shaking with fury.

She wanted to beat at him with her fists. She wanted to scream at him, the way she had three years ago. She wanted to force him to listen while she recited all the likenesses between Flynn and Johnny.

Drawing in a deep breath, Pride deliberately began the process of calming herself. If Flynn was so determined to ignore the truth, none of those things would convince him.

Tomorrow, she told herself. She would tell him tomorrow. If that didn't run him off, nothing would.

Yes, she had better do it tomorrow. If Flynn kissed her again, she might go up in flames and seduce him. If that happened, what were the odds that she'd get pregnant again?

But if she told him Johnny was her son, not Gloria's, Flynn might take to his heels, thus saving her from the proverbial fate worse than death.

Pride smiled to herself in a shaky way. What a way to go.

*

Flynn Sutherland opened his office door and peered out at his secretary. Killeen Ross had the *Chronicle* open on her desk, avidly reading a column.

Grinning, Flynn walked out and bent over Killeen's shoulder, aware that she hadn't heard him, so engrossed was she in her reading.

Flynn studied the column. The slightly out-of-focus photograph of Tracy Eric, dark-haired and beautiful, followed the "Single Mommy" header. Beneath the photograph, the column bore the title, "Home Again Memories."

"Listen to this, boss," Killeen said. " *Now that the last permanent man in my life is gone forever, I wonder how my son will feel when he learns of the father he has never had a chance to know. Will he blame me? Will he blame my former lover? Will he understand the short-lived love that brought him into being?*" Killeen heaved a tragic sigh. "I was wondering that very same thing. I found out last night my father is terminally ill. He was the one real, dependable man in my children's lives. Without him, who will they have to look up to?"

Flynn skimmed the remainder of the article, wherein Tracy Eric examined the feelings her father's death had brought into being, and most of all, the effects of that death upon her too-young-to-understand son, who had never known his grandfather.

Tracy's son would never know a grandfather's love now, and she mourned that fact. Flynn read the passage and mourned along with Tracy, then told himself he was a fool.

Once more, he wondered why he hadn't gone ahead and married Pride. Then he reminded himself it wouldn't have made any difference, since Pride had suffered a miscarriage.

He had realized last night when he watched her face as she spoke to his father that Pride had suffered. Whatever else she'd been lying about, Pride had been pregnant. Or had thought she was pregnant.

Now, he would probably never have a chance to present his parents with a grandchild to love and spoil. He regretted that almost as much as the thought that he'd never have a child of his own to love and spoil.

"*'I'll always wonder what would have happened if my lover had lived up to his promises,'*" Killeen read aloud. "*'Would my father have accepted my son if he had been what my Dad considered a "legitimate" baby? It's too late now for anything except regrets.'*"

"Her father was an idiot." Disturbed by the similarity of Tracy Eric's situation to Pride's, he scowled down at the columnist's photograph. "That baby was still his grandchild. What kind of man could ignore that?"

"He was probably a religious freak," Killeen said.

Flynn considered, frowning. Pride's father hadn't been a religious freak. Alan Donovan had impressed him as a self-righteous jerk who had approved of Flynn because of Morgan Sutherland's wealth and social standing.

He straightened and rubbed the back of his neck. He'd thought Pride was exaggerating when she said her father thought she wasn't his daughter.

Perhaps Pride hadn't exaggerated about certain other assertions she'd made.

Flynn drew in a bracing breath. "Well, did you glean anything from today's column that helps with your children?"

Killeen got out a pair of scissors and began cutting out the column. "You bet I did. She hit the nail on the head when she wrote about the promises her lover failed to live up to." She clipped viciously. "Men are weasels. They'll say anything to get a woman to bed with them. Or into the kitchen cooking and cleaning for them. Not a single thought for the children." She whacked at the paper with the scissors. "They don't seem to realize that there'll come a day when God is going to ask them how they treated the little ones assigned to their care."

On that note, Flynn retired to his office, shaken. If Pride had given birth to the baby, then had presented herself and the baby before him, would he have accepted the role of father?

Probably, Flynn realized wryly. He was a sucker for babies.

He wished he'd had the chance to prove it.

A disturbance in the outer office gave notice that Pride and her cousin had arrived, with the four children in tow. Flynn opened his office door, eager to see Pride again.

Dressed in jeans and a loose-fitting blouse, she stood beside Killeen's desk, nodding over the Tracy Eric column. Although she still looked too white and frail in his opinion, the casual attire pleased him. She looked more like herself.

Gloria bent over one of her dark-headed children, gently scolding. Two of the children had fanned out, in search of something to get into trouble with.

The fourth child regarded him out of huge, brown eyes from Pride's arms.

"Flynn's," Johnny said, holding out his arms.

Flynn glanced at his wrist involuntarily, but his sleeve hid the watch. That meant Johnny wanted to be held by him. The idea was both touching and irresistible.

"May I take him, Pride?" he asked.

Pride started and looked up. "Of course. Behave yourself, Johnny. If possible." She transferred Johnny to his arms.

"Impossible," Killeen said. "He wouldn't be a normal little boy if he behaved himself."

"True," Pride agreed. "He's had quite a morning already."

Flynn listened, grinning, as Pride described a hilarious incident wherein Johnny had applied black shoe polish to a pair of Gloria's white leather tennis shoes.

"He's still got it under his fingernails," Flynn said, spreading one of Johnny's small hands for inspection.

"Flynn's," Johnny squealed, in triumph.

Too late, Flynn realized he had inadvertently exposed his watch to Johnny's covetous view. He almost dropped the struggling child, who literally fought to get his hands on the watch.

"That kid loves your watch, boss," Killeen said. "You wouldn't withhold a treasure like that from a little bitty child, would you?"

"Flynn, if you dare to give him that watch, I'll choke you with it," Pride said. "Take it off and put it in your pocket."

Flynn's incredulous gaze focused on Pride while he balanced the wriggling Johnny on his arm. "Pride Donovan, this is between me and Johnny. Kindly stay out of it."

"Now, Flynn, recollect that I have yet to return your watch stem. If you let him get his hands on that watch again, there's no telling what he'll swallow next. Maybe the face, with all those pretty little flags. Or the crystal. Now that would require an operation to remove it, I think. Glass shards..."

"It's shatter-proof," Flynn said, straight-faced.

"Hah. Don't you believe it," Pride said. "Would you like me to tell you what he did to an 'unbreakable' plastic bowl?"

Flynn, laughing, bounced Johnny in his arms to distract him and slipped the watch off his wrist and into his pocket.

"Flynn's," Johnny complained, searching Flynn's wrist.

Flynn watched as the child's small hands explored his forearm, where a band of white skin signified the former presence of the watch. The feel of the little hands on his arm aroused feelings of fierce possessiveness in him. What would he give to be able to call a boy like this one his son?

He looked up to find Pride's gaze focused on his face.

"Flynn's?" Johnny demanded.

Flynn blinked. Johnny's frustrated little face hovered six inches from his.

"Flynn's has been put up for the duration," Flynn said gravely. "Your aunt's orders."

Killeen blinked and looked puzzled.

Pride laughed outright.

"Gloria would be the first to say she has no wish to ruin her afternoon rushing him to the hospital for ingested watch gears," she said.

Johnny didn't care about that.

"Flynn's," he wailed, and dissolved into loud sobs.

"Johnny," Pride said, in stern tones. "If you mean to carry on like that, you won't get to go on the sailboat. I'll have to take you home. Alone. With me."

In the face of the sinister implications of this speech, Johnny sniffed his way into silence.

"Don't listen to her, old buddy," Flynn said. "I won't let her take you home to the dungeon in chains."

Johnny sniffed and focused trusting brown eyes upon Flynn. He crawled higher in Flynn's arms and fastened his small arms around Flynn's neck.

"Sailboat," he said.

"That's right," Flynn said, unaccountably thrilled. "Ever been sailing before, old buddy?"

Johnny watched him with grave interest.

"Never mind. Everyone has to start somewhere. I'll let you raise a sail yourself. Ever hoisted a sail before?"

"Sail," Johnny said, in tentative tones.

"You're going to love it," Flynn promised. "Just watch yourself. Otherwise, the wind will catch you and you'll land in the water like your Aunt Pride did one day."

"Aunt Pride?" Johnny repeated, glancing at Pride.

"Has she been lying again and telling everyone what a great sailor she is?" Flynn asked, grinning at Gloria.

Gloria, who had been keeping well out of the discussion, smiled back. "She said we should put on life jackets and sit still and let you do all the work, because you will anyway."

Flynn laughed. "True. I'm not used to sailing with a crew."

"Is that what we are?" Gloria asked, with foreboding. "A crew?"

"Right," Flynn said, with considerable satisfaction. "This is my first mate." He indicated the big-eyed Johnny. "Anyone refusing to follow orders will walk the plank."

"Careful, Flynn," Pride said. "Your crew is liable to start planning a mutiny."

Flynn felt a tugging at his trousers leg and looked down. Eric stood there, asking silently to be taken up into Flynn's arms with Johnny.

He bent to lift the older child then faced Pride, laughing.

"That isn't likely," he said. "In another few minutes, I'll have won most of the crew over to my point of view."

Chapter Five

By the time Flynn became willing to put the two little boys down, Pride wondered if he'd try to adopt both of them from Gloria. It lifted her spirits immeasurably to see Flynn so obviously enchanted by her son and by Gloria's children.

"You'd better come to the office a few minutes, at least, Pride," Flynn said, at last. "There is one thing in particular I need to give you."

Whatever it was, Pride thought, scowling, she didn't want it if it came from her father. Why spoil a perfectly good day?

Flynn watched her. "What on earth do you think it is?"

"I really haven't the faintest idea."

"All right, men, I'll be back out in fifteen minutes. If there are any signs of mutiny in my crew, I'll keelhaul the lot of you. Got that?"

Johnny thought keelhauling sounded like fun. He grabbed Flynn's leg and looked up at him, laughing.

"Especially you," Flynn promised.

Jealous, Eric dealt Johnny a surreptitious poke in the ribs. Johnny let out a howl and swung wildly at his tormentor. The two little boys clinched and rolled across the floor, yelling imprecations at each other.

Pride started across the room then glanced at Gloria, who was also starting forward. They exchanged grins and halted.

Flynn grasped each little boy by his collar and hauled them apart.

"If you want to sail on my boat," he said, with stern emphasis, "you have to fight the sails, not each other. Crewing a sailboat requires teamwork. Is that clearly understood?"

Eric said meekly, "Yes, sir."

Johnny sniffed and pouted, hanging his head.

"I don't want to come out here in fifteen minutes and find the two of you fighting again. Understood?"

The boys indicated their understanding.

"Pride, will you step into my office, please?"

Flynn kept a stern eye on the children as he ushered Pride into his office until he shut the door behind him. The moment the door closed behind him, he grinned at Pride.

"Well? Do you think I rate as a strict disciplinarian?"

"That was fantastic," Pride said, pleased. "I didn't know you had it in you."

"I have lots of hidden talents. You'd be amazed."

"I'm sure I would." Pride covered her smile. "What is it you want to show me, Flynn?"

Flynn went to his desk, where a folder awaited his attention. He opened it and pulled out a long, white, sealed envelope with her name on it and handed it to her.

"It was in with your father's legal documents." He reached into the folder and began laying out several legal documents in a row along the desk. "These are ready for your signature. If you like, I'll explain each one to you. Killeen is a notary. When you're ready to sign, we'll have her in."

Pride stared at the documents. "Am I signing away my birthright or something?"

"This is your birthright," Flynn said. "This one is the deed to the house in Anahuac. This one transfers several blocks of stock to you. This one is the deed to five beach cabins in Crystal Beach that your father kept as rent property."

Pride swallowed. She had no idea her father owned beach front property.

"Do I have to sign these?"

"Yes, if you wish to inherit the property. However, you can, if you so desire, refuse to inherit."

"What would happen then?"

"Your father's next-of-kin would inherit. I'd have to scrape around in your genealogical tree and find out who that would be."

Pride sighed. She could have told him the person he wanted was, at the moment, getting into trouble of some sort in his outer office.

"Never mind. I'll sign."

The property would be Johnny's inheritance in the end. Her son would be assured of a good education and property of his own when he reached adulthood.

Flynn smiled at her and used his intercom to request Killeen Ross's presence. She came in, bearing her notary book and seal and laughing.

"Johnny has discovered the pleasures of my computer keyboard," Killeen said. "He's banging away on it."

Pride groaned.

"Obviously a talented kid," Flynn said. "Just be sure he doesn't eat some of the keys."

Pride signed the documents, conscious all the while of the wild clacking of a computer keyboard in the outer office. When she had finished, and Killeen affixed her signature and the notary seal to the papers requiring it, Flynn nodded at the white envelope Pride had laid on his desk.

"I don't know what's in it," he said. "I think your father was going to tell me, but he died before I could come to him."

Pride opened the envelope and extracted the document it contained. "It's my birth certificate, and an old letter from my mother to him."

She studied it in silence, conscious of Flynn's regard as she read the names of Alan Donovan and Elizabeth Bernard Donovan. There was nothing on the certificate she didn't already know, and she wondered why on earth her father had retained her birth certificate among his legal papers.

The old letter, written before her parents had married, very likely contained the answer. She replaced the letter and birth certificate back in their envelope and tucked it in her tote. She didn't dare read the letter until she was alone, if then. Maybe she would have Gloria read it.

"I think he was trying to tell you something," Flynn said.

Pride looked at him, conscious of a swirl of conflicting emotions in her heart and an equally conflicting swirl of thoughts in her brain.

A loud wail sounded from the outer office. Pride recognized Tracy's voice, and an instant later, heard Gloria putting down the insurrection.

"I think I'd better change clothes so we can go," Flynn said. "Otherwise, the children may kill each other."

"You're so right," Pride said. "Believe it or not, all that fighting means they're learning how to get along."

"True," Killeen said. "All too soon, they'll quit speaking to each other. Mine are at that stage."

"How old are your children?" Pride asked, interested.

"Thirteen and fifteen. The thirteen-year-old is jealous of the fifteen-year-old, and the fifteen-year-old thinks the thirteen-year-old is too gross for words. It's an interesting development, after all the fighting they did the previous twelve years." Killeen smiled warmly at Pride and left the office.

Pride filed away the fact of Killeen's single parenthood of two teens. Writers tended to collect people who were experts in a wide variety of fields.

"What are you thinking, Pride?" Flynn asked.

She looked up to see his warm, brown gaze on her face.

"I was wondering how Gloria was going to get along when her kids get into their teens," she improvised.

"She seems to have her children well-in-hand. Want to step outside while I change?"

Pride went and plucked Johnny off Killeen's computer. She held him in her lap and sat down to engage Killeen in a discussion of Tracy Eric's thoughts as applied to single parents of teenagers.

Flynn appeared, now clad in old khakis and a plaid shirt, and Pride studied him from behind Johnny. He looked like the Flynn she remembered, far more enticing to her eyes than the suit-clad lawyer.

He led the way to the parking garage, carrying Sylvia and Johnny both, while Pride and Gloria herded Tracy and Eric.

"We're going to Galveston," he said. "Who wants to ride with me?"

All the children wanted to ride with Flynn, which would be possible if all the safety seats designed for children were transferred to Flynn's Bronco. Grinning, Pride personally saw to the transfer. It was high time Flynn received an overdose of eager children. They'd keep him hopping all the way to Galveston.

She and Gloria rode alone in Gloria's SUV and experienced incredible silence. Pride drove and enjoyed herself both in watching the scenery and in conducting an uninterrupted conversation with her cousin.

"He seems so intelligent," Gloria mourned. "How can he possibly think Johnny is my son?"

"When Flynn gets an idea into his head, it's a major impossibility to get it out," Pride said. "I've decided to go ahead and tell him the truth tonight. Not that it'll change anything," she added. "He'll still think I was running around with someone else."

"What would be interesting might be Flynn's parents' reaction to Johnny," Gloria said, in thoughtful tones. "I'll lay a bet Flynn looked just like Johnny when he was two."

"Children look alike at that age. They're all adorable."

"True. Is Tracy Eric going to explore her feelings upon seeing the father of her child once more?"

"Tracy Eric has already done so," Pride said, in dry tones.

"With Killeen Ross reading every word Tracy writes let's just hope Flynn doesn't catch sight of that particular column."

"Maybe I'll mail it to him, all underlined."

Pride laughed. "Now that would really be interesting."

"I still think you ought to have told him two years ago, when Johnny was born," Gloria said. "However, no one ever listens to me."

"At the time, I couldn't have handled it." Pride gave her cousin a wry smile. "If Flynn had made one of his scathing remarks, I might have brained him. Then Johnny would lose his mother as well as his father."

"Do you know what would really be funny?" Gloria began to chuckle. "What if Johnny starts screaming for 'Mommy,' and you automatically come running?"

"Nothing would change," Pride predicted. "Mark my words, Flynn would assume it was because I'm playing favorites among your children."

"I can't wait to tell Eddie about this," Gloria said, shaking her head.

They sped along the Gulf Freeway, heading directly into downtown Galveston. Salt water marshes surrounded the highway as they approached the bridge across the bay that would take them into the city.

They reached the city of Galveston and followed Flynn to the marina. Pride pointed out various historically important, Victorian structures and savored the once-familiar surroundings as she parked beside Flynn's Bronco.

She hadn't been here since the morning she'd driven to this same marina and sat all day waiting for Flynn, who had taken his boat out to get away from her. When he had finally docked, salty and weary, she had been standing on the dock. While he tossed his lines to a dock official, she had shouted that the problem was not going to go away if he ran from it.

Flynn had absolutely congealed with fury. The scene that had ensued was one she preferred not to remember.

Pride gripped her hands on the steering wheel and fought off the memory as Flynn climbed out of the Bronco and cast a helpless glance their way.

"He looks shell-shocked, poor man," Gloria said, and hurried toward him.

Pride closed her eyes and sought to blank her mind, only to discover Flynn standing beside her when she opened them. His narrowed gaze told her he remembered also.

"Forget that," he said, and lifted her bodily from the car seat. "From now on, we start fresh. Pride, will you marry me?"

Her mouth fell open. "What?"

"You heard me. I still love you, as much as ever, it seems. Marry me, and I'll make everything up to you. I promise."

Her mind went blank. She struggled to remember exactly why she should say no, which in itself warned her that she was in deep, deep trouble.

"Say yes," Flynn urged, and kissed her.

Pride found herself caught in a vortex of thundering, roiling emotions. She trembled in his arms, and for an instant veered between a longing to strike him and a longing to make love with him. He deepened the kiss, holding her against him so tightly he left her in no doubt how much he wanted her.

He lifted his head at last. "This is what I should have said to you when I found you waiting for me on the dock."

Jolted back to reality, Pride turned her face away. "That would have been nice. Too bad it didn't happen that way."

"It can happen that way now." Flynn crushed her against him and kissed her temple. "Just say yes."

"I can't, Flynn. There are," she hesitated when her scattered wits refused to supply any reasons, "some things that I have to tell you. Things you need to know."

"And are any of these 'things' something that would make us ineligible to marry?" He tensed.

"If you mean, is there another man in my life, the answer is no." Pride got her hands between them and pushed away until she had managed to put two inches between them. "But they could very well change your mind about marriage."

"In that case," Flynn said, "maybe you'll let me take you someplace to eat tonight so we can discuss the wedding."

She waited a moment before replying, while her pulses settled and her mind cleared somewhat. "Maybe I will. In the meantime, I need to help Gloria corral the children."

Now that Flynn no longer touched her, she let her gaze pass over boats of all descriptions that lined the marina docks while her emotions settled. She noted sailboats with short masts and tall masts, motor yachts, fishing yachts with flying bridges, and many smaller motorboats. She had missed the sights, sounds, and the smells of diesel fuel, fish, and salt that marked the marina.

Much to her amazement, she suddenly realized Flynn had erased her one bad memory of the marina.

"Let's go," Flynn said, recalling her attention.

Sounds from inside the Bronco indicated that the children feared being left behind. Pride and Gloria grinned at each other as they opened the car doors and began extracting children.

"Did you have a peaceful drive?" Pride asked, all innocence, and placed Johnny in Flynn's arms.

"Surely you jest." Flynn ruffled Johnny's hair. "I had to quell three major clashes and two minor skirmishes. I didn't know they could still reach each other in those seats."

"My husband and I have been considering walls between each seat," Gloria said, straight-faced. She cradled Sylvia in her arms. "Pride and I had such a quiet, peaceful drive."

Flynn watched Pride take Eric's and Tracy's hands. "I'll bet you did. I can see motherhood is a vastly underrated profession."

"Too true," Pride struck in. "Let's go, Flynn. The kids are fed up with driving. They're ready to see some boats."

"This way," Flynn said. "I called ahead and asked them to be ready for us."

The children loved the marina. Eric asked one question after another, and Johnny was so busy craning his neck to see the boats, he nearly fell over Flynn's shoulder.

"This one is ours." Flynn stopped beside a large, blue and white motor yacht bearing the name, "Farah."

Pride studied the yacht. "Who's Farah?"

"I was afraid to ask. Come aboard, folks." He urged them up the boarding ladder. "I can't wait until you see the galley, Pride. You'll love it."

This boat was Flynn's business, Pride decided, assessing the size of the boat. What did he care whether she loved it or not? It had to be at least a forty-footer, which meant the cost would start somewhere around two or three-hundred-thousand dollars.

The moment she stepped on the deck, she mentally raised the price. This boat had been planned with luxury at sea in mind. The aft deck resembled a patio, and there was even a swimming platform complete with ladder. Gloria promptly tried out a chair, holding Sylvia in her lap, and her two older children ran to stand at the rails.

"Look around at your leisure," Flynn told them. "Come on, Pride. Let's take a tour."

Flynn looked like a little boy with a wonderful new toy. Pride, reminded forcibly of Johnny, looked away when he took her hand and urged her down the companionway and into the luxurious cabin.

She stared around at the plush, pale-blue-and-teak decorated salon, with its wrap-around sofa and glass coffee table. "Are you bucking for admiral of the shrimp fleet?"

"Skipper of this vessel will do, thank you."

"This is an admiral's private quarters at the very least," Pride said. "Or a billionaire's. Who else would have the ridiculous sum required to buy this boat?"

"Have a little faith in my negotiating abilities," Flynn protested, pulling at her hand. "It belongs to one of my clients. He's getting a divorce and wants to unload it fast."

Johnny, riding high on Flynn's shoulder, turned his face toward her, and Pride was again struck forcibly with the resemblance between their two faces.

"Is that so? I've seen enough, Flynn. It's gorgeous."

"You have to see the aft stateroom." Flynn towed her down a few steps. "It's the master bedroom."

Pride stepped into a room that looked like a luxury bedroom, with a queen-sized bed in the center and two teak night stands on either side. She stared into mirrors that made the room seem even larger, investigated an actual walk-in locker, and studied a private head that rivaled any bathroom on land.

"I think I'm more a sloop kind of person," she said. "I'd be so nervous in here, I wouldn't sleep a wink."

"Nervous?" Flynn protested. "What on earth about?"

"I'd keep wondering when the bank was going to foreclose."

Flynn, she saw, was quite taken by this dream of a boat. She reminded herself once more that it was none of her business. He certainly had the money to pay for it if he wanted it.

Naturally, the galley lived up to Flynn's promise. It had not only a microwave oven, but a conventional oven and an electric refrigerator as well. Pride, who had been accustomed to cooking over an alcohol stove on Flynn's sailboat while strapped into a harness designed to keep her from being thrown about while she cooked, professed herself overwhelmed.

"Well?" Flynn demanded. "What do you think?"

"It's wonderful." She waved her hand in a dismissive gesture. "Buy it. You aren't interested in listening to reason."

"Don't you like it?" Flynn asked, hurt.

"Like it? Who wouldn't like it? It's a mariner's dream."

"I knew you'd like it," Flynn said, satisfied. "Come have a look at the forward stateroom."

Pride surveyed the dinette opposite the galley. "I don't need to see anything else. Hold still, Johnny."

Johnny struggled to get down. He had seen enough from Flynn's shoulder and wanted to go exploring on his own. Flynn kept his gaze on Pride and gently set Johnny on the floor. Johnny promptly took off into the forward stateroom.

They followed, and Flynn smiled, watching Johnny peer beneath the king-sized bed and examine the drawers on the bedside table.

"You ought to close down your apartment and move to the boat," Pride said. "It would be criminal to maintain an apartment in addition to this."

Flynn laughed. "You'll need more closet space for your clothes."

"Not me. If I lived on a boat like this, I wouldn't need any clothes other than the ones I'd wear on the boat."

"Don't you think Gloria and Eddie would enjoy going out on the Gulf with us for a week or two?"

"With or without the kids?" Pride asked.

"With," Flynn said, with equanimity. "The dinette sleeps two, and the salon will sleep the rest. This boat can handle eight adults, so the kids should be a cinch."

"I don't think you know what you're asking for," Pride said, smiling at his enthusiasm. "Have you ever been cooped up with four little children in a very small area?"

Flynn touched her face with his fingertips. "No, but the fact that I'm willing to try ought to say something in my behalf."

Pride turned her face away, as if to study one of the bedside tables. "It does. You should receive a medal for valor. And for an exceptional number of dramatic rescues performed at sea, when one or more of the kids decides to go swimming without parental permission."

"Do you really think they would?" Flynn's expression of disappointment was almost ludicrous. "Can't they be trained not to go near the deck rails?"

"You have just mentioned the operative word. Training."

"Oh." Flynn smiled. "Well, I'm new at training children. One of the experts will have to show me how it's done."

Pride struggled to smile, stricken suddenly by the realization that she would love to watch Flynn attempting to train his own son not to go near the deck rails.

"Just watch Gloria or Eddie for about five minutes." She felt suffocated. "You'll receive better training than if you bought and read several books on child care."

"I have a feeling you're right." Flynn tugged at her hand. "Come on. Let's go check out the deck."

"I can't believe you've given in like this. No one ever thought you'd trade in your sails for a motor."

"I'll never trade in Whisper," Flynn objected. "It's just that there comes a time in a man's life for other options. I now have other people to think about."

Did he mean her? Pride glanced at him, met his watchful gaze, and turned scarlet.

"Gloria and Eddie will appreciate the thought," she managed.

"Maybe we'd better go check out that closet in the aft stateroom one more time," Flynn said, grinning. "If you think it's too small—"

"Too small? The only way it would be too small is if you're a Saudi oil sheik."

"I'd never go for a yacht I can't handle myself," Flynn protested.

"I know. That's why you'd better be happy with that wonderful walk-in locker and quit worrying about how much space your clothes are going to take up. Stash them in nets, the way we used to on your sloop."

"I don't want you having to compromise anymore," Flynn said.

Johnny, having checked out the stateroom, took off at a dead run toward the salon. Once more, Pride's brain refused to keep up with Flynn's tongue.

She blinked. "Compromise? What on earth do you mean?"

"Never mind. I just want you to be comfortable when we take the new boat out." He was silent a moment, guiding her back to the salon. "Here. Want to sit down and try it out?"

Pride wondered how much of the conversation she had missed. Flynn assumed she would accompany him out on the Gulf when he took the new boat out. What else did he assume?

The salon was a spacious room that resembled a living room, except for the fact that Flynn's head was within several inches of touching the ceiling. Several comfortable chairs, a teak and glass coffee table, and a real sofa lined the small space.

They sat down together on the light-blue sofa. Flynn put his arm across the sofa behind her, and together they watched Johnny experiment with the wheel at the inside control station, which was located beside the sofa.

"Comfortable, sweetheart?"

"Very." Pride sighed with pleasure.

She glanced up at the windows that partially encircled the elegant sitting room. Light poured in, giving the boat's interior a cheerful, light-filled atmosphere. Her only objection to Flynn's sailboat had been the dark interior of the cabin.

"I knew you'd love it," Flynn said, pleased. "It'll take me a few days to complete the paperwork then we can take her out."

"Flynn." Pride sought for caution. "If you buy this boat and it springs a leak or something, you'd better not claim I insisted that you buy it."

"Absolutely not. I had already decided on it before I ever told you about it."

She felt his fingers tangling in her hair and leaned forward.

"Johnny, stop twisting the wheel that way. Turn it gently, or you'll break it."

"He won't break it," Flynn said, grinning. "Let him play. We're supposed to be testing the child-worthiness of the boat."

"I don't know if any boat can withstand the onslaught of four children," Pride said. "Where is Gloria? She's supposed to be exploring this dream boat along with us."

"Gloria is being tactful, I think," Flynn said.

"Is that so? I'd better go find her. There may be a child overboard."

"Sit still, Pride." Flynn tugged her hair. "I want to talk to you." He kept a hand in her hair, and lightly massaged her neck as he tried to get her to meet his gaze. "I wanted to apologize for hurting you the way I did three years ago."

"Thank you." She closed her eyes, unable to meet his steady gaze. "I accept your apology."

"I was so hurt, I never thought about you and your feelings the way I should have. I'm truly sorry, Pride. I see now that you were hurt far worse than I thought I was."

He massaged her scalp gently in a vain attempt to turn her face toward him. Pride found the gentle touch as seductive as his voice and fought to keep her attention on Johnny.

"If you believed I was two-timing you, then naturally you wouldn't think about my feelings," she said.

"I cared about you. Common decency should have led me to check on you. You might have needed someone."

Pride stared down at dark blue pile carpet. It had taken weeks to overcome her hurt, to accept the situation with grace and humor, and to become capable of planning for the future.

"I wasn't in any danger of giving in to despair," she said, "but thank you for the thought."

His hand tightened in her hair, and he tilted her head around to face him.

"I hurt you a lot worse than I thought," he said, in grim tones. "Were you counting on me that much?"

He probably meant that she had counted on him to rescue her from her own folly in sleeping with another man who couldn't, or wouldn't, take care of her, she realized.

She answered him truthfully. "I suppose I must have. A young woman often has the idea that somewhere she'll find a man who's willing to shoulder all her burdens and straighten out all her problems." She gave him a genuine smile. "It takes a few years for her to learn that she really has no one she can count on except herself. But we still go on taking chances. Otherwise, there would be no children with two parents to rear them."

Flynn watched her, eyes narrowed. "If it's any comfort to you, I've often wished I'd gone ahead and married you anyway."

"It's a good thing you didn't. My life would have been miserable, and so would yours." Unable to face him another minute, Pride broke loose from his light grip on her hair, leaving several long, blond strands clasped between his fingers, and stood. "If I had a miscarriage, you'd feel trapped and angry. If I had the baby, you snipe at me for the remainder of our lives together, no matter how much like you the child looked. No, Flynn, your ditching me was the best thing that ever happened to the both of us."

She whirled and headed toward the companionway, reminding herself that Flynn might yet turn out to be a carbon copy of her father.

Flynn grabbed her arm and jerked her back. "Dammit, Pride, I am not your father."

"No, but in that situation, who's to say you wouldn't behave exactly like him? My father didn't even have the extra bonus of thinking he was sterile."

She fought him, but Flynn held onto her. He pulled her into his arms and stared into her furious green eyes.

"Let go of me, Flynn." Her voice shook.

"I don't think so." He shook her lightly. "Pride, I—hey."

Pride followed Flynn's startled movement and looked down.

Johnny, his brown eyes filled with tears, glared up at Flynn with his upraised fist ready to strike again at Flynn's leg. His lower lip quivered with hurt.

She forgot her anger and knelt, holding out her arms. It was criminal of her to forget Johnny's presence like this.

Johnny flung his small body into her embrace, and Pride clasped him to her, murmuring softly in his ear. "Everything is all right, darling. Flynn and I were just talking."

Johnny gave a mighty sniff and burrowed his face into her breast.

"Let's go up on deck and look at the boats, okay? I hear one going by in the water. If we get there quickly, we can see it."

She struggled to her feet, cuddling Johnny, and walked toward the companionway, conscious of Flynn behind her.

By the time she reached the deck, Johnny had forgotten his fear in the excitement of racing to the foredeck in time to watch a fishing yacht head out of port toward the open Gulf. They took up a position along the rail and waved at the three fishermen occupying the flying bridge of the passing yacht.

"Pride, I'm sorry." Flynn stood beside her, watching her steadily. "I didn't mean to upset you. Or Johnny."

"I wasn't thinking," she admitted, turning back to watch the passing yacht. "I'm sorry he hit you."

Flynn came closer. When she made no movement away, he took her hand and held it.

"It served me right," he said. "Do you think he'll ever forgive me?"

"Ask again after we're off this boat and on your sailboat."

He lifted her hand to his lips. "What about you? Will you ever forgive me?"

Pride looked away. "Of course, Flynn. You don't even have to ask."

"Great." He smiled whimsically. "I still want to marry you, you know. No matter what it is you intend to tell me tonight."

Chapter Six

Pride swallowed hard and turned her gaze toward a slowly passing yacht. By the time 'tonight' arrived, she would probably be searching for a way of putting off the moment of revelation a little longer.

What an idiot she was. So much for being mad because Flynn didn't realize Johnny was his son. Now, she feared Flynn would be furious when he learned the truth. So furious, he would rescind his offer of marriage and sue her for custody of Johnny.

"Time will tell," she made herself say in light tones.

He smiled with wry humor. "Unless, of course, you intend to tell me that you had the baby, and he's alive and well and living with his father."

"As a matter of interest, why would that kill your desire to marry me?" she asked, genuinely curious.

"Because then I'd have to kill the guy so I could have both you and the baby," he said, astonishing her. "I made a big mistake when I let you walk out of my life three years ago."

Pride stood absolutely still, staring blindly at the water before her. Did Flynn mean that he wanted a son so much he would be willing to accept her baby even if he believed some other man had fathered the child?

Nothing made sense anymore.

She felt certain of only one thing, however. Until Flynn knew and accepted that Johnny was his son, she could not even think about marrying him.

The man was diabolical. He was deliberately messing with her mind.

"This is some boat, isn't it?" Gloria approached, still carrying Sylvia. "It's amazing how well they used the space."

Pride relaxed slightly. "It's an art."

"Eric Boudreaux, get away from that rail," Gloria called. "If you want to go sailing, you have to obey the rules. The rules say, stay back from the rails."

Excited chatter from Gloria's three children ebbed and flowed as they raced from one side of the deck to the other. Pride noted the lack of comment from Johnny and looked down.

"Johnny," she shrieked.

Johnny, who had climbed through the rails to peer down at the water, tumbled headfirst off the deck at her cry and splashed down into the water some five feet below.

Pride, panicked, flung a leg over the rail.

"I'll get him," Flynn said, blocking her.

Pride, shaking with fright, hung over the rail and searched for Johnny's blond head beneath the surface of the oil-slicked, dark water. The little boy surfaced, coughing and flailing at the water with his hands.

Flynn leaped over the rail, hung by his hands for a moment until he spotted Johnny surfacing, then dropped lightly into the water beside the child. He lifted Johnny high above the surface and glided easily through the water to the nearby dock.

Pride forgot everything, including the frightened tears that rolled down her cheeks, as she raced across the deck to the boarding ladder. Seconds later, she stood on the dock to receive Johnny when Flynn held him up to her. She collapsed onto the wooden walkway and hauled Johnny, dripping and coughing, into her lap, almost crushing the child in her arms.

Flynn pulled himself onto the dock and knelt beside her while she held Johnny and alternately scolded and hugged the little boy while she cried.

"Take it easy, Pride," Flynn said. "He just thought he'd see how close he was to the water."

Pride looked at him through tear-filled eyes and laughed. "He has to learn everything the hard way. You see?" she asked the little boy. "Now you're all wet, so we're going to have to go home instead of go sailing."

Johnny, safe and brave, set up an incoherent protest.

"Don't be silly," Flynn said. "It's a warm day. He'll be dry in no time. We can take off his clothes and let him run around the boat naked until they dry."

Pride focused on Flynn. His shirt and trousers clung to him, and water dripped from his heavy, sun-bleached hair. He looked wonderful to Pride, especially after saving her son, so she covered her emotion by joking.

"Is that what you're going to do?" She tilted her head up to find her cousin. "Get ready for a thrill, Gloria."

"I'm used to being wet when I sail." Flynn laughed and looked up at the boat rail, where Gloria and the three dark-headed children had gathered. "Johnny's fine. Just a little wet. Come on, Johnny. Let me carry you for a little while, okay?"

Johnny regarded Flynn with a serious demeanor but raised no objection to riding in Flynn's arms. Flynn reached down a hand to help Pride to her feet.

"You're almost as wet as Johnny," he observed. "Would you like to take off your clothes and—"

"Shut up, Flynn Sutherland," Pride interrupted. "If you hadn't been so heroic just now, I'd kick your kneecap."

"Heroic?" Flynn repeated, and laughed. "Oh, Lord. If the others behave like Johnny, I ought to get plenty of opportunities today to show off my gallantry. I'd better change."

"Do that," Pride said. "We can hang your clothes off the halyards to dry."

Gloria, herding the other three children, met them on the dock beside the boat.

"Here's your errant son," Flynn said, placing the puzzled Johnny into Gloria's arms. "He's wet but wiser, we hope."

If Flynn had been given to analysis, Pride thought, he might have wondered at the incredulous glance Gloria gave him. Knowing Flynn, he probably interpreted the stare as thankfulness that Johnny was all right.

She shot a grin at Gloria, and Gloria shook her head and rolled her eyes.

Johnny reached for Pride, and Pride thankfully clasped his small, beloved body to her breast.

She pinched his cheek and hissed, "Don't you ever get near that water again."

Flynn spoke to a dock official, who regarded Flynn's waterlogged state with interest.

"Our boat is ready," Flynn said. "Let's stop by the car and get our lunch sacks."

"Don't tell me you packed a picnic lunch," Pride said. "I thought I was going to have to cook."

"Wait till you see what I have in the sacks," Flynn said mysteriously. "We'll have a late lunch, once we get out into the Gulf."

"Is this where I get to see Pride in that cute little harness she described to me?" Gloria asked.

"We'll see," Flynn said, grinning. "Come on, Johnny. You're getting Aunt Pride wetter than she already is."

Gloria grimaced, but Flynn didn't notice. He took Johnny from Pride's arms and Sylvia from Gloria's and led the way to his Bronco, where two paper sacks sat in the rear. Pride and Gloria each took a sack and followed Flynn to a slip where a fairly large, single-masted sailboat was tied to the dock.

"All ashore who are going ashore," Flynn declared and instructed the children where to sit.

He went below to put up the sacks then returned with a handful of life jackets, two bottles of sun screen, and two hats. He insisted that everyone present don life jackets, including himself, although Pride knew he usually dispensed with that precaution when sailing by himself. She felt greatly relieved, knowing Flynn was setting an example for the children by wearing a life jacket.

Pride and Gloria rubbed the children down with the lotion and tied hats on themselves. She applied sun screen to her own pale skin and thankfully tied a hat over her hair. The excitement of going on Flynn's sailboat once more had been so intense, she forgot the precautions against sunburn.

She studied him appreciatively. He had shed his wet clothes and wore only a pair of swimming trunks. His tanned, muscular chest and arms rippled in a way Pride found utterly enticing, although she tried hard not to stare.

Pride sat in the small cockpit beside Gloria and held Johnny in her lap while Flynn, working alone, prepared to hoist the mainsail.

While he worked, he lectured his captive audience on the physics of the wind as interpreted by boat sails. All four pairs of children's brown eyes followed his every move when he untied the lines holding them to the dock and started the boat motor, which would serve to get them away from the dock and headed away from the wind.

"Any questions?" He cut the motor and hoisted the sail.

Wind filled the mainsail and the sloop leaped forward. Silence reigned. The boat sliced through the water under wind power, silent and smooth.

"I'm so glad you asked, Eric." Flynn smiled at the silent, big-eyed little boy. "The jib is the sail we're going to hoist next. Come over here, and you can help me hoist the jib."

"Me," Johnny shouted, and struggled off Pride's lap.

At that, all four children shouted for a turn and gathered around for Flynn's lesson in jib-hoisting. They listened avidly as he described the aerodynamic effects of the two sail-design.

"I can't believe you're going to trade all this for a motor yacht," Pride called.

"Nothing doing," Flynn said. "I'm hoping to form a two-boat family. Hold this rope, boys. You two girls hold this rope."

Flynn did most of the work, but the four children had a wonderful time thinking their efforts had hoisted the working jib, especially when the boat responded with a noticeable increase in forward speed.

"Now, everyone sit back and let the skipper take over," Flynn said.

Flynn enjoyed teaching the children, Pride saw. The thorough wetting hadn't affected him in the least.

She watched her son. The warm sun had already partially dried his clothes. In another half-hour, he wouldn't show the effects of the dunking at all. He wouldn't even catch a cold, knowing Johnny. He was a wonderfully healthy little boy.

"I wouldn't believe this if I weren't seeing it for myself," Gloria said, in low tones. "No one but a mother has hysterics when her kid falls in the water."

"Maybe he thinks you're burned out," Pride said, grinning. "Four of them would probably do that to a woman."

"Sure. Just wait till Tracy or Eric, or, God forbid, Sylvia, goes overboard. Then he'll see hysterics."

"Okay, kids," Flynn said. "Come here and sit down. This is where we let the wind take us out."

Flynn joined the two women, keeping his hand on the wheel as they sailed briskly out of the yacht basin toward the open Gulf of Mexico. The children followed, fascinated by the boats they passed. Flynn lectured them about the differences between fishing yachts, luxury trawlers, ketches, sloops, and cutters.

The further out into the Gulf they went, the bolder the children grew. Soon they ventured around the deck and fought over whose turn it was to handle the wheel.

"It's my turn." Flynn effectively ended the small battle. "We're about to heave to and eat lunch. Who wants to help me lower the sails and set the anchor?"

"With that many helpers, it's a wonder the poor man can do anything," Gloria commented.

"This can't go on any longer," Pride said, in a low voice. "He's taking me to dinner tonight. I'm going to tell him then."

"The sooner, the better. I hate to say this, Pride, but I'm just about at the point where I'm going to deny publicly that Johnny is my son."

"I can understand why." Pride laughed. "Not many mothers would care to claim him after he'd ruined a pair of white shoes with black shoe polish."

Flynn lowered the sails and set the anchor, then hustled everyone below into the boat's tiny cabin. He had stopped at a take-out delicatessen and picked up a variety of sandwiches and desserts, which he set out on the dinette on paper plates.

Gloria professed herself fascinated by the small galley, and the harness the cook had to wear when the boat was under sail. Even the single berth in the forward area of the small cabin caught her interest.

Pride turned away, unable to remain in the cabin another minute. That berth was where Flynn often made love to her, and she would always remember everything that had happened there.

She glanced surreptitiously at Flynn, discovered his gaze upon her, and knew he remembered, also.

She grabbed a tuna sandwich and hastened back on deck.

"What's wrong, Pride?"

Flynn joined her, at the side of the boat. She hung her legs over the edge and kept her back to him, but he sat down beside her and hung his legs over beside hers.

"Nothing's wrong. It's such a beautiful day, I thought I'd come up here and enjoy it."

"You never did like the dark cabin on this boat, did you?" Flynn gave her a sympathetic smile. "You'll like the new boat a lot better."

"I thought you hadn't bought it yet."

"I'm afraid I'm guilty of thinking it's already mine. I've even picked a new name for it."

"Take care it doesn't get sold to someone else," Pride recommended.

Flynn reached absently into his pocket, fished out his watch, and reclasped it on his tanned forearm. It looked so dear and familiar Pride had to turn her face away.

"Are you sure you want to wear that?" she asked. "Johnny is sure to see it."

"He hasn't forgotten his desire to taste the nautical flags?"

"His memory is worse than an elephant's," Pride said, in solemn tones.

"I'll take it off if he notices it," Flynn said, smiling. "I want to keep tabs on how long we've been out."

She stared out over the gray-green Gulf waters. The afternoon sun was warm on her skin, in spite of the sun screen she'd applied liberally, and she turned her face up to it.

"Are you making your freckles bloom?" Flynn asked. "Good. I've really missed those freckles."

Three dolphins broke water nearby and leaped along. Smiling, Pride pointed toward them.

"Pride," Flynn said.

She automatically turned her face toward him.

The next instant, he took her in his arms. He used one hand to tilt her chin up and the other to lock her against him while his lips took hers in a hot, hard kiss.

Startled, Pride gasped. The moment she parted her lips, his tongue entered her mouth and stroked hers. The steady, salty wind blew his hair into her face, and the scent of his favorite citrus aftershave still clung to him in spite of his unplanned swim.

Every one of Pride's five senses came awake to the fact that the man holding her so tightly was Flynn, whom the very marrow of her bones had once responded to.

And still did, she admitted to herself, in spite of everything. She trembled, and her arms went around his neck.

Flynn felt her acceptance. He brought her body even closer to his and deepened the kiss. Gasping for breath, Pride responded with everything inside her. Her fingernails dug into his back, and her breasts flattened against his chest. If she could have melted into him, she would have done it.

"Flynn's," an aggrieved, childish voice exclaimed.

Pride started and broke the kiss to peer over her shoulder. Johnny stood about three feet from them, lower lip protruding, clearly unable to decide between hitting Flynn with his upraised fist or latching onto the coveted mariner's watch. His mouth and chin were smeared with chocolate.

"He isn't hurting me, darling." Pride held out her hand to the child, although Flynn still retained her in his embrace. "Come give me a kiss."

Johnny glared suspiciously at Flynn.

"He's very protective of you, isn't he?" Flynn said, grinning. "I don't think I'd better turn my back on him."

"Johnny, come here, darling. You don't want Flynn to think you're mad at him, do you? When he's been nice enough to bring you sailing on his boat?" She moved, with slow, deliberate motions, out of Flynn's arms.

Johnny rushed to her and buried his face against her shoulder. Pride put her arm around him and kissed him. From this protected position, Johnny peeped at Flynn, who smiled at him.

Johnny jerked his face back into Pride's shoulder. She patted his back gently and whispered in his ear.

"Why don't you give Flynn a kiss, darling?"

Johnny considered. He peeped once more at Flynn.

"Go ahead," his mother prompted.

Flynn watched, interested, and Pride grinned wickedly at him. She had no idea how Flynn felt about receiving kisses from a child who had been indulging in what looked like chocolate pie, but as far as she was concerned, he had a right to kisses from his own son.

Johnny relented at last. He took his face from Pride's shoulder, walked a few steps to Flynn's side, and put his small arms up.

Flynn leaned down gravely, and Johnny put his arms around Flynn's neck and planted his sticky mouth on his father's cheek.

"Thank you, Johnny," Flynn said. "You're quite a man, aren't you?"

"Man," Johnny said, pointing at Flynn.

"That's right, and so will you be one day."

"Flynn's," Johnny said, and grabbed for Flynn's wrist.

"You said it," Pride informed the child. "It's Flynn's, not yours. Get your grubby little paws off it. Flynn doesn't want chocolate pie all over his arm. Let's go below and wash your hands and face."

Johnny planted his feet and protested, but Pride prevailed. She swung him up and tucked him beneath her arm. His protests served only to make his mother more determined to restore him to pristine condition.

Gloria supervised her brood at the dinette. "It's amazing how well space has been utilized. Everything you need is in this single, tiny space."

"I used to get claustrophobic at times." Pride scrubbed at Johnny's face and hands at the deep sink. "Teak interiors are beautiful but dark. I spent every minute I could on deck."

"You're going to love my new boat," Flynn said.

Pride glanced up, surprised. Flynn stood in the companionway smiling at her, although the lines around his mouth showed white and something about his expression betrayed tension, as if he had just received a serious shock.

"Come back on deck," Flynn said. "Deck is the only place to be on a sailboat."

The next instant, he looked completely normal again, and Pride decided she had been mistaken.

"This boat was designed for dedicated sailors like Flynn," Pride told Gloria, as they followed the children on deck. "The cabin exists to sleep and cook in. Otherwise, you stay on deck."

"I can see why you loved it." Gloria looked out over the Gulf. "I'd love to be out here alone with Eddie."

"No, you wouldn't," Pride said, laughing.

"Well, maybe for—Tracy, get away from that rail—one day. It would give us time and incentive to work on another little Boudreaux."

Pride laughed and glanced around the deck. Johnny followed Flynn to the stern and appeared to be reviewing his arguments for obtaining Flynn's watch. Tracy explored the port side of the boat. Eric and Sylvia explored the starboard side.

"Let's get somewhere in the middle where we can keep an eye on them all," Gloria suggested. "If I know Eric, we should have a man overboard any time now."

"Johnny will beat him to it," Pride predicted.

But the first person overboard wasn't either of the two boys. Little Sylvia, as fascinated by the water as Johnny had been, crawled to the edge of the deck to look down at it. While her mother's eye was to port, she slipped beneath the deck rail for a closer look and tumbled into the Gulf.

Eric gave an incoherent shout. Pride jerked her head around and noted at once the direction of the little boy's gaze.

"Flynn," she called.

"Sylvia." Gloria screamed and rushed toward the rail. She tripped over a pile of rope and sprawled out on the deck with a heavy gasp.

Flynn raced toward them. "Help Gloria. I'll get the baby."

Before he reached the rail, Eric leaned over to try and reach his sister. He tumbled headfirst into the water beside her.

Gloria screamed again, despite her winded state, and struggled to her feet with Pride's aid.

"Don't worry. Flynn will get them," Pride said.

Flynn vaulted over the rail and disappeared.

Tracy and Johnny, attracted by the shouts, ran to join them at the rail.

Johnny saw his two cousins in the water having what looked like fun. He dove beneath the rail and splashed down beside Flynn, shouting, "Flynn's."

"Tracy," Gloria yelled. She grabbed the little girl and dragged her back from the rail. "He'll never save them all."

"Yes, he will." Pride spoke in a deliberately calm voice. "Don't forget, they're wearing life jackets."

Tears poured down Gloria's face, but what Pride said came true. Flynn, taking his time, gathered the three children into the circle of his arms while they bobbed in the water around him.

The children loved it. The unplanned dunking turned into an opportunity to swim and play in the water, and they made full use of it.

"Take her, Pride." Flynn held up Sylvia.

Gloria almost went over the rail herself reaching for her daughter.

"Here's Johnny," Flynn said, in imitation of the announcer on the old Johnny Carson show.

Pride reached down and snagged her son. She hauled him, dripping and unrepentant, onto the deck beside her.

"I'll take Eric around to the stern and climb the ladder," Flynn said.

Pride agreed and proceeded to scold Johnny thoroughly, not that she expected him to listen. Johnny had enjoyed his impromptu swim.

Smiling, she carried Johnny to the stern and reached out a hand to help pull Flynn aboard. This time, she hadn't even worried when the children went overboard. She knew Flynn would rescue them.

Gloria, clutching Sylvia beneath one arm and towing Tracy,

rushed up. She seized Eric, scolded him, and applied the palm of her hand to his bottom several times.

"That's what you need," Pride told Johnny. "If you even go near that rail again, you're going to get it."

"They were enjoying themselves down there," Flynn said, smiling at the still-distraught Gloria.

"I'm sure they were," Gloria said. "I knew I'd be totally unnerved if one of them went overboard. I don't care what Pride says about life jackets."

"I'm a great savior of overboard children," Flynn protested, although the white look appeared around his mouth once more. "Pride prepared me ahead of time. So far, the only one I have yet to save is Tracy. Would you like to hop overboard and let me rescue you, sweetheart?"

"Absolutely not." Gloria maintained her clutch on Tracy's shoulder. "My nerves have had it."

Tracy giggled and hid her face against her mother's leg.

"In fact, I'm thinking seriously about locking them all in the cabin," Gloria said.

"Don't be mean, Gloria," Pride said, grinning. "You're robbing Flynn of his chance to be a hero."

"Sorry, Flynn," Gloria said. "If I weren't so upset, I'd kiss you. You have singlehandedly restored two of my most precious possessions to me, but, if it's all the same to you, I'd rather not put you to any more trouble."

"She means, 'Let's go the heck home,'" Pride interpreted.

Flynn smiled at the slender, dark-headed woman. "Your wish is my command. I'm sorry about this, Gloria. I should have been helping you watch them."

"It wasn't your fault," Pride said. "I warned you about this when you offered to take us out."

"So you did," Flynn said. "All right, crew. Let's get to work hauling in the anchor and hoisting the sails."

Pride, watching him, noted the faint frown that marred the smoothness of his brow. Added to the pinched, white look around his mouth, Flynn looked as if he had received a severe shock.

Perhaps he had finally put two and two together without reaching his usual five.

On the other hand, maybe it just meant he was pondering a problem presented by his sails.

*

Flynn focused his mind on hoisting his sails to catch the wind in the direction he wanted to go and tried to ignore the thoughts that bombarded his brain.

In spite of himself, he compared Gloria's reaction when Sylvia fell overboard with Pride's reaction when Johnny fell overboard at the marina. He also recollected that Gloria had thanked him for rescuing two of her most precious possessions, not three.

It couldn't be, he told himself. Surely Pride would have said something.

A vision of the four children as he had first seen them lined up on his office sofa arose in his mind. Two brown-eyed, dark-headed little girls, one brown-eyed, dark-headed little boy, and one small brown-eyed, blond boy.

It wasn't possible.

But during the ride back to the marina, he found himself unable to think coherently on the subject at all. His mind turned in circles, racing between hope to denial. But he would say nothing if it killed him. He was through speaking before he thought and saying things that hurt Pride.

He breathed deeply. Pride went to his head the way she always had, and he could hardly wait until the evening when he could kiss her again.

He felt starved for her kisses. He'd been starving for three years, and he hadn't even known it. Tonight, he thought. Tonight he would take Pride someplace quiet where they could talk. Then he would ask his questions.

He looked at Johnny, asleep in Pride's arms, and refused to let himself hope.

Just because Johnny had blond hair... Just because Pride treated the little boy like she would her own son....

It couldn't be true.

But somehow, he knew it was.

Chapter Seven

Flynn did not know how he managed to dock his sloop and tie up to the dock. He knew the motions in his sleep, he supposed, because he certainly felt like a sleepwalker, especially when he looked at Pride.

She smiled at him and got slowly to her feet, careful not to jostle the sleeping child in her arms, and walked toward him so he could help her step from the boat onto the dock.

He feasted his eyes on the picture she made, with Johnny snuggled against her breast and his face buried in her blouse. If it turned out not to be true, he wondered if he could live with the disappointment. He took Pride's hand and tried to look as if he had not just had the wind literally knocked out of him.

He found he couldn't end the day just yet.

"Let's stop in at the café for something to drink," he suggested. "You and Gloria could use a good cup of coffee to drive home on."

"And how." Gloria, herding Eric and Tracy and carrying Sylvia, gave him her hand and stepped onto the dock beside Pride while he lifted the two children off the boat and set them on the dock beside her. "I'll need two cups if I'm to drive back."

Pride smiled at her cousin. "Sailing and salt air are the two greatest soporifics known to man. We'll sleep well tonight."

Flynn led the way and held the door of the café open for them. When he had them settled at a table and drinks ordered, he wondered if he could let Pride leave. Sitting across from her, he could hardly take his eyes off her and Johnny, even though all he could see of Johnny was the back of his blond head.

"There you are," a familiar voice said from behind him. "I hoped to catch you when you docked, but we ran into traffic."

Flynn started and turned. "Dad? What are you doing here?"

Morgan and Bettricia Sutherland came toward them, casually dressed as befitted an afternoon at the marina. Bettricia wore a flowered sundress and white sandals, and Morgan sported a green polo shirt and plaid trousers.

"We came to invite Pride and her cousin to have coffee with us, of course," Morgan said. "If she won't come to us, then naturally, we will have to come to her."

"We hope we're not intruding." Bettricia looked at Pride with a kind of hopeful anxiety. "But we didn't want to miss the chance to visit with you."

Pride smiled at them, a genuine smile of welcome and liking. "That's very flattering, but it wasn't at all necessary. I intended to pay you a visit sometime in the next few days."

Flynn refused to let himself ponder the implications of that statement. He rose at once and drew up a chair to seat his mother, then introduced Gloria and the two older children.

"Gloria is holding little Sylvia, and Pride is holding Johnny," he finished, indicating the back of the little boy's dark blond head.

And his mother smiled and said, "His hair is exactly the color of yours when you were little, Flynn."

Morgan studied the child in Pride's arms. "So it is. Your children are beautiful and extraordinarily well-behaved," he said to Gloria, and seated himself beside her. "You must be very proud of them."

Gloria thanked him. "They're well-behaved because they're tired, and two of them are asleep. But we expect mayhem shortly when we get back on the road."

Then the moment Flynn both dreaded and anticipated arrived. Johnny stirred in Pride's arms, then jumped awake in the manner of active little boys. He sat up and turned to take in the new arrivals, and Pride turned him to sit in her lap.

Johnny's wide-eyed brown gaze fell on Morgan's left wrist. The big, diamond-encrusted Rolex watch his wife and son had given him for Christmas one year shot off sparkling shards of multicolored light in the afternoon sunlight.

"Flynn's," Johnny squealed, and launched himself across the table like a bottle rocket.

Pride caught him, but the table rocked dangerously and the various liquids splashed in all directions.

Bettricia Sutherland sat frozen. Not even the contents of Pride's cup of coffee liberally splashing her flowered frock distracted her attention. Then she quietly closed her eyes with a faint keening sound and slumped back in a dead faint.

Morgan Sutherland also sat in stunned silence and stared at Johnny's face. "You didn't have a miscarriage."

"I never said I did." Pride cast Flynn a defiant glance. "Johnny, sit still. Just look at this mess you've made."

"Flynn's," Johnny wailed, stretching out his little hands toward Morgan's left arm.

"It doesn't belong to you, and you can't have it," Pride said. "Excuse me, please. Johnny and I need to have a little talk in private."

Flynn supposed his brain had taken a sabbatical. He could not seem to think. He could only observe what happened. But he managed to get to his feet in time to draw Pride's chair out for her, and to catch his mother before she slid from her chair to the floor.

Pride ignored the pandemonium at the table and carried Johnny, bawling at the top of his two-year-old lungs about "Flynn's," toward the restrooms.

Flynn turned his mother over to Morgan and went after Pride. This was not the way he wanted this to happen, but at least he no longer needed to question her about Johnny's parentage.

He stood outside the door of the women's restroom and found his wits slowly returning. Amazing, how his parents had recognized Johnny for what he was at once, whereas it had taken him an entire two days, since he had first observed the little blond boy in Pride's arms at Judge Donovan's funeral service.

He closed his eyes. Pride probably thought he was the biggest dunce in Texas. No doubt he was.

He was also the luckiest man in Texas, maybe even in the whole United States. He had a son. He was Johnny's father.

At the moment, Flynn did not know what emotion would win out, but joy, fury, and a kind of stunned surprise crashed through him at intervals.

He gathered himself. Johnny's wails subsided and he knew Pride would emerge with the child at any moment.

What, he wondered, did a man say to a woman at a moment like this? Flynn searched his brain and came up with precisely nothing.

But after three years of loneliness and wondering about Pride, he knew what not to do. No matter what, he would not accuse her of hiding Johnny from him. He realized Pride thought she had told him the truth multiple times.

The door to the women's restroom opened and Pride emerged, carrying Johnny.

"Why didn't you tell me at once?" he demanded.

"Tell you what?" Pride gave him a bland stare that dared him to say another word.

He remembered his promise to himself and shut his mouth on the accusations he wanted to yell at her. He had done enough of that three years ago, and he knew Pride probably remembered every nasty thing he had said.

"You and Gloria must have gotten a good laugh out of this situation," he said, through gritted teeth.

She stepped around him, smiling resolutely. "Actually, Gloria can't believe it. But she does agree that Johnny is just like you, very tenacious once he takes an idea into his head."

"Flynn's," Johnny said, as if to prove the assertion.

Flynn stared at the child. Johnny studied him then studied his bare wrist with obvious disappointment, but he reached out his small arms to his father.

"May I take him?" Flynn felt as if he'd been sucker-punched.

"Of course. Just hold onto him when he sees your father's Rolex again."

"Thank you." Now he felt humbled, because the gift she handed over to him was so much greater than anything he had ever expected.

"This doesn't change anything," he said. "I'm still picking you up this evening. We need to talk about this."

She raised delicate brows and smiled. "I'll be ready."

"One thing, Pride." He stopped her when she took a step toward the dining room. "When were you going to tell me? Or were you ever going to tell me?"

Her green eyes met his with all the honesty he had once associated with her. Once more, Flynn felt as if he had been sucker-punched.

"Tonight," she answered. "I told Gloria I'd had enough of waiting for you to notice how much Johnny resembles you. In case you're interested, I have his birth certificate and all the papers from my medical checkups and hospitalization to show you."

"I'm interested." Flynn held Johnny against his chest, savoring the feel of the child's sturdy, little body and the tickle of the little boy's soft hair against his neck. "I'd like to see all those things, but not tonight. Tonight, we'll talk."

She nodded and turned away. "We'll be lucky if the manager doesn't ask us to leave. Johnny caused quite a ruckus in there."

"Nothing a few dollars can't fix." Flynn smiled and hugged Johnny—his son. "Is this sort of thing a common occurrence?"

"Actually, he's usually a lot better behaved than this." Pride led the way back to their table, where two older people in particular awaited them with incredulous anxiety. "That watch of yours started his manners on a downhill slide, and I'm afraid your father's Rolex is likely to demolish what's left of them."

"If we're not careful, Dad is likely to buy Johnny his own Rolex," Flynn said, chuckling.

"Not if I have anything to say about it." Pride gave Johnny a boding glance. "Let him eat pennies like a normal child. Diamonds are too rich a diet for little boys."

He soaked in the joy in laughing with Pride over their son's antics and smoothed his palm over the little boy's shoulder. In that moment, he knew exactly what steps he would take next.

*

Pride found Morgan Sutherland rising to his feet by the time she returned to their table, pulling out her chair as if she was a princess.

"Pride, why didn't you tell us?" He stared at Johnny, riding in Flynn's arms, in a covetous way. "We would never have let you go off alone if we'd known."

"Thank you." Pride meant it. "But it was Flynn's right to tell you. I'm sure he would have done so by tomorrow."

She deliberately skated over the three years in between, when Flynn had believed she was either lying about being pregnant or lying about who the father was.

"Oh, Pride, darling, I don't know what to say to you," Bettricia said. "He's beautiful, the very image of Flynn at that age. He even has Flynn's dimple."

"What dimple?" Flynn grimaced and sat down beside Pride. "If I ever had a dimple, it's long gone now."

"At Johnny's age, you had one on your left cheek just like Johnny's." Bettricia watched Johnny in a yearning way, and Johnny looked back, interested. "Hello, darling. Can you say 'Grannie'?"

"Grannie," Johnny said in his clear child's voice. "Flynn's."

"Yes, I'm Flynn's mother," Bettricia said. "That makes me your grannie. Can you give Grannie a kiss, darling?"

Johnny examined this request and found it doable. He stood on Flynn's thigh and leaned forward to pucker his little mouth in

Bettricia's direction. She presented her cheek, and the little boy smacked loudly at it.

"What a smart boy you are," Bettricia said in besotted tones. "Look at him, Morgan. He's got your eyes."

"Flynn's" Johnny yelled and stretched out his hands toward Morgan's left arm. "Mine."

"No, Johnny, it is not yours," Pride said, without much hope of convincing anyone. "Sit down before you make another mess. Flynn, you'd better—"

Flynn moved too late to stop Johnny's lunge for Morgan's watch, but he did manage to prevent disaster by snatching the little boy in mid air and standing.

"What is it he wants?" Morgan asked, in tones of wonder. "Is he saying, 'Flynn's'?"

"He recently developed a taste for Flynn's mariner's watch," Pride said. "He thinks your Rolex would make a tasty substitute."

Morgan promptly unclasped the watch and held it out. "He can't hurt one of these things. Let him play with it a while."

Pride blocked the transfer, holding out her hand in warning. "That's what Flynn thought about his watch, until Johnny ate the stem. No, Johnny. It isn't yours."

"Flynn's," Johnny howled, at the top of his voice.

"Are we going to go have another talk in the restroom?" Pride asked, in her sternest voice.

Alas, Johnny had somehow divined that the two new additions to his circle of acquaintances desired to spoil him, and he took full advantage. He gave Morgan a heartrending, teary-eyed look and moaned, "Flynn's."

"Here, Johnny." Morgan placed the big, gold watch in Johnny's hands. "You can give it back when we leave."

"Flynn's." Johnny signified his happiness by leaning toward Morgan with puckered lips. "Grannie."

"Grandpa," Morgan corrected, with tears in his eyes.

Pride exchanged glances with Flynn and said nothing more. Clearly, Morgan thought Johnny worthy of the expensive plaything.

With Morgan and Bettricia present, she couldn't talk to Flynn about anything other than commonplaces, but she would not for the world have missed watching Morgan and Bettricia Sutherland cooing over their grandchild, or Flynn's proud face as he held the child on his lap and watched him systematically experiment with Morgan's Rolex watch.

When she and Gloria at last insisted the children needed to get home and bathe, she had all the difficulty she expected in detaching Johnny from Morgan's expensive watch.

"Let him keep it, Pride," Morgan said. "He won't hurt it."

Flynn gently pried the little boy's fingers from the watch. "That's what you think, Dad." He exchanged a gleeful glance with Pride. "I'm afraid you're already missing three of the diamonds around the bezel."

"Flynn's," Johnny protested. "Mine."

"He ate them?" Morgan took the damp watch in a gingerly fashion and examined it. "So he did. Well, they won't hurt him. Here, Johnny. It's a present from your Grandpa."

Pride thought it prudent to intervene. "No, Johnny, it is not yours. It belongs to Grandpa, and it's time to give it back to him. It's getting near your bedtime."

Johnny filed a preliminary motion of protest, but Pride overruled him with the firm tones he had learned to respect.

"She's right, Morgan," Bettricia said, with brisk emphasis. "We can't spoil him, much as we'd like to. We'd better get home too. If Pride brings him and these other little ones to see us, we need to child-proof the house."

Morgan brightened as he wrapped his wet Rolex in a paper napkin. "So we do. You will bring him, won't you, Pride?"

The humble request shook Pride to her soul. She knew they

sought to show her they had no intentions of going against her wishes, but somehow, she had not expected to feel this deep gladness.

She sought to analyze it logically, but the feeling eluded her, until she realized she was glad that someone besides herself cared about Johnny and would stand in her place if something happened to her.

In that moment, she felt a great burden roll off her heart.

*

When Flynn's knock sounded at the door that evening, Pride was in the middle of the ritual designed to coax the children into having a good night's sleep.

Before she could put Johnny to bed, Pride had one more duty to perform. Flynn deserved a formal introduction to his son. She invited him inside and asked him to sit down on the white sofa for a few minutes while she fetched Johnny.

"Your son wants to tell you good night." She led Johnny to the sofa. He wore blue pajamas and regarded Flynn with intense interest.

"Now, darling." Pride knelt on the floor beside him. "Do you remember how I explained to you that Uncle Eddie is Eric's and Tracy's and Sylvia's daddy, but that he isn't your daddy?"

Johnny nodded with solemn fascination, still watching Flynn.

"Flynn is your daddy. Your very own daddy. Come give Daddy a good night kiss, darling."

Flynn appeared both stunned and touched by the action. He sat, unmoving, as Pride urged Johnny forward.

"Flynn's," Johnny commented in undertones and scanned Flynn's bare wrist.

"That's right, darling. You're going to be Flynn's little boy, and he's going to be your daddy. Do you know what that means?"

Johnny stared at Flynn with enormous penny-brown eyes. "Daddy?"

"That's right. Flynn is your very own daddy. Come and give Daddy a kiss, darling."

Johnny approached and studied Flynn fearlessly before trying to climb onto his lap. Flynn looked so bemused he didn't move to help the child for a moment.

He came to himself with a start and reached for Johnny, bringing the child close. His lashes veiled his dark eyes, and he laid his cheek against Johnny's silky, blond hair. His mouth tightened, as if he wanted to cry, and Pride backed off.

She waited a moment, but Johnny seemed content to rest in Flynn's arms. Flynn held him, burying his face against the child's soft mass of dark-blond hair. Pride slipped from the room and joined Gloria in tucking the other children into bed.

Flynn, toting Johnny high in his arms, appeared at last in the doorway to the bedroom where the two women had added two cots to the double bed. The two little girls had the bed, while Johnny and Eric each had a cot. Three pairs of Boudreaux brown eyes fastened expectantly on Flynn.

"The adult male," Gloria said. "Your duty is clear, Flynn. Get busy."

"What?" Flynn still looked as if the entire world had gone upside down all of a sudden.

"You owe everyone a goodnight kiss," Pride specified. "Don't think you'll get away from here tonight without contributing to the public good."

She had to smile at the dazed way Flynn stared at the waiting children.

"Do I start with Johnny, or end with him?" Flynn wanted to know.

"It doesn't matter in the least," Pride assured him. "The only thing necessary is that no child is passed over."

Flynn placed Johnny on his cot, and Pride tucked the little boy's teddy bear in beside him. Flynn leaned down and kissed him, and Johnny kissed back with a loud smacking of his lips.

Flynn would probably have liked to linger over Johnny's bed, but he valiantly went to each of the little Boudreaux children in turn, kissing small foreheads and patting the covers around their shoulders.

"My daddy sits on the bed," Eric stated.

"This bed isn't quite big enough to hold both you and me," Flynn said with suitable gravity.

Eric gazed up solemn silence. It was clear that he felt this was a minor infraction in the rules of being a daddy.

While Flynn fulfilled the duties of the sole adult male, both Pride and Gloria kissed each child in turn.

"There's more?" Flynn wore the dazed expression of someone who has strayed into the middle of a battle.

"Unfortunately, yes." Pride laughed at him. "It's now time for prayers."

Flynn swallowed, to Pride's delight, but he was game. She had to hand it to him.

"You get to be in the middle." She grabbed his hand.

Gloria grabbed his other hand, and the two women pulled him down to kneel on the floor between them. This signaled the children to kneel beside their beds, with folded hands and closed eyes.

"My daddy says the prayer." Eric looked expectantly over his shoulder at Flynn.

Flynn stared at Pride in silent pleading.

"Flynn is new at this," Gloria pointed out. "Aunt Pride and I are going to say the prayer tonight."

Gloria led a prayer which asked blessings on the household, on each person in it by name, and especially on one Eddie Boudreaux, currently on a drilling rig in the Gulf of Mexico. Pride added to

Gloria's petition, mentioning Flynn's parents for Johnny's benefit.

"All right, everybody," she said, upon closing. "In the bed. Eyes closed."

The four children leaped back beneath their covers and squeezed their eyes shut. The three adults tiptoed from the room, and Gloria flicked the light switch off and partially shut the door. She and Pride remained at the door for a moment, listening.

"They're tired, thank God," Gloria said. "I do believe they're going to go to sleep with no trouble."

"Glory be." Pride pretended to wipe her forehead. "Come on, Flynn. There's coffee in the kitchen."

"I'd like to talk privately with you, if you don't mind. Gloria, I promise I'll have her back in an hour. Now that I've seen it for myself, I can understand why Pride didn't want to leave you alone for long."

Gloria laughed. "Don't let her snow you. I'm accustomed to dealing with lots of little children. What's one more?"

"It depends on the identity of said one more," Pride said. "Let me get my purse."

She fetched her purse and wondered whether she should load it with a brick, just in case, then chuckled at the thought. Poor Flynn was in no condition to fight at the moment.

Flynn walked her to his Bronco and helped her step inside, then stood looking at her a moment. Dusk fell rapidly, but the light was still good enough for him to study her figure in the pink cotton dress she wore.

"I see now why you've gotten so thin," he said.

Pride gave him a challenging look. "I've been on a diet. When you knew me, I still had a certain amount of puppy fat."

"Don't hand me that," Flynn said in rough tones. "You've been too keyed up to eat. I remember how you always got when you were wound up over anything. You have been nervous, haven't you? For the past three years."

Pride considered denying it, but Flynn wasn't above tackling Gloria about it. Gloria's loyalty to her cousin extended only so far. If Gloria thought it would bring relief to Pride, she'd spill all to Flynn.

"A child is a tremendous responsibility," she temporized. "It won't be long until you'll probably wish you hadn't learned about Johnny."

"Don't think that, Pride," Flynn said. "Don't ever think that." He closed the door and came around. "Other than you, Johnny is the greatest thing that's ever happened to me."

Pride said nothing. There was no safe reply she could make.

Flynn glanced at her and smiled as he started the engine. "You don't believe me. One of these days, no matter how long it takes, you will."

Pride forbore replying. Flynn's statement sounded uncomfortably like a vow. She saw no sense in saying something that would increase his determination.

"You've been thinking ahead about Johnny's future, haven't you?" he asked.

"Yes. I was all he had, you know, except for Gloria and Eddie. That's why I specified you as Johnny's legal guardian in my will."

"Your will." Flynn turned his head to stare at her and almost drove into a ditch. "When did you make your will?"

"Before Johnny was born, of course. Childbirth is supposed to be a natural procedure, but one never really knows."

He concentrated on the street ahead in silence for a moment.

"Who was with you when Johnny was born?" he asked.

"Eddie and Gloria." She disliked the set look of Flynn's jaw as he asked the question. "Eddie is a world-class expert in coaching a woman through natural childbirth. Gloria was almost nine months pregnant herself. She sat on the sidelines yelling encouragement from time to time."

Flynn smiled also, but lines of strain appeared at the corners of his mouth. "I wish I had been with you."

"No, you don't, Flynn. I wasn't the best of patients. Pain isn't my forte, and I gave poor old Eddie hell."

Flynn didn't find that as amusing as Pride had hoped he would. His expression, or what she could see of it in the shadowy evening light, grew even more strained.

"I should have been with you," he said.

Pride said nothing. God knew she wished he had been.

"Tell me about it," he said suddenly. "I want to know everything you can remember, starting from the first labor pain."

"I don't remember the first pain." Pride watched Flynn's hands as he guided the Bronco into the parking lot of a small restaurant. "I had just conceived the idea for a column, and I was hard at work on the first column when I suddenly realized I was cramping, and that it had been going on for some time."

"I remember." Flynn's knuckles showed white on the wheel. "When you were writing, you forgot everything."

He'd said he wanted to know, Pride reiterated inwardly. "I figured it was nothing, since I wasn't due for another week. So, I got up and stretched a bit and got back to work. In another hour the pain got so bad, I knew something was up."

"You need a keeper." Flynn gripped the steering wheel.

Pride shrugged. "When I stood up, I knew the time had come. I called Gloria, and she located Eddie and sent him over. He hauled me to the hospital, and Gloria joined us after she took Eric and Tracy to her mother's."

"What happened then?" Flynn parked the car, shut off the motor and remained in place, staring straight ahead.

"Nothing." Pride smiled. "That's when I nearly went crazy. The pain got worse and worse, and Eddie kept telling me to pant until I threatened to sock him in the eye. He said socking your coach in the eye wasn't allowed, and I yelled a lot of unrepeatable stuff. Eddie finally had to back off and coach me from a distance."

She glanced over and found Flynn's face turned toward her.

"Go on." Flynn didn't seem to find the story amusing.

"After hours and hours of that, Johnny finally managed to get himself born, with very little help from me," she finished.

"Tell me about it," Flynn instructed.

"What do you want to know, Flynn? By the time Johnny was born, I was in pretty bad shape. I don't do pain, especially prolonged pain, and that's what childbirth is. I was thankful when it was over."

Flynn frowned. "What did he look like?"

"He looked flattened and red and mad, but I thought he was the most beautiful creature on earth. In fact, I fell asleep admiring him."

"When did you get to go home with him?"

"The next day, thank goodness. I bounced back fast."

She said nothing about the three weeks she'd spent with Eddie and Gloria, while she learned to care for her baby, and the struggle she'd made to breastfeed him. Flynn, after one glance at her, forbore pressing for more information. He unbuckled his seat belt and got out slowly, still frowning.

She smiled. "Johnny is already turning you into an old man."

"Between the pair of you, I should be pushing ninety in about two more days." Flynn came around and helped her out. "I suppose you must have gotten ready for this gradually."

The pressure of Flynn's warm hand at her back felt both comforting and familiar. For a moment, she hovered in danger of dumping all her burdens on Flynn.

"I suppose I did." She edged out of his range.

"Come back here." Flynn seized her arm and tucked it in his. "One more action like that out of you, and I might really go crazy."

"All that was over three years ago."

"No, Pride, it isn't over." He studied her face. "Not by a long shot. You just haven't realized it yet."

They followed the hostess to an unoccupied table. Flynn seated her, and when she claimed she wasn't hungry, he ordered two cups of coffee and two dishes of vanilla ice cream, along with a slice of pumpkin pie for Pride.

"You used to love pumpkin pie," he said, when she protested. "You're much too thin. The only way to gain a little weight back is to take in a few more calories."

"Since I couldn't be rich, I was trying for thin." She pleated her napkin then smoothed it out.

"I told you." Flynn smiled at her. "You're rich now, so you can afford to gain some weight. Eat it for me, Pride. I want to see you looking like yourself again."

"Well, I think I look better now." Pride straightened and gave him a defiant look. "What do you want from me, Flynn? It ought to be obvious to you by now that I want you to know Johnny and to have a chance to be his father. What else do you want?"

Flynn replied simply, "You. I want us to be a family, you and Johnny and me."

"You had me three years ago, Flynn. You just didn't want me." She propped her chin on her hand and stared at the table top. "I hoped you would ask me to marry you before you took off for Europe." She shrugged. "Look how that turned out.

"If you want to know the truth, I was stalling because I knew I was going to have to reiterate the part about not being able to give you children." He watched her a moment. "I know it sounds ridiculous now, but I wasn't looking forward to making that speech."

"You're right. It does sound ridiculous."

"Try and understand, Pride. A man doesn't relish feeling something less than a man."

"If you think you can explain to me what siring children has to do with being a man, please try," Pride said, exasperated.

"I don't think you'd be very receptive of any explanation can give you," Flynn said. "A man's ego is bound up in things like virility."

"Virility is very different from fertility," Pride pointed out. "In fact, I'd be the first to state that there's nothing wrong with your virility. Or your fertility either, for that matter." She added, in tones of annoyance, "If you're willing to propose now because your mind has been set at rest on those points, you can forget about it."

"We made a child together. Don't you think he deserves a traditional family structure with two parents to watch over him?"

Pride waited while the waitress set coffee before them and said nothing.

"What will it take to convince you I'm serious?" he asked.

"I want you to know Johnny. I'm not going to be doing things to circumvent your rights as a father. Can't you let it go at that? You don't have to be married to me to have free access to your son."

"I'm not talking about Johnny," Flynn said. "I'm talking about us. You and me. It should have been obvious to you that I was trying to get you back before I found out about Johnny."

"I wouldn't know, Flynn," Pride said. "I've had a lot on my mind. Lots of things passed right over my head while I was waiting for tonight to come."

"Was it this afternoon?" Flynn laughed. "It seems a lifetime ago. I've become a different man."

She glanced up. "You have?"

"Sure, I have. I've become a father."

Chapter Eight

Flynn saw that Pride liked that statement. "Yes, you are a different man, once you become a father," she agreed.

He watched her add a generous dollop of milk to her coffee. "Have you read the letter your father gave you yet?"

Pride glanced up in surprise. "Not yet. Things were rather hectic when we got home this afternoon. The children didn't want to settle down and go to bed." She concentrated on her coffee cup once more. "Maybe tonight."

"Don't put it off too long," he said. "Which brings me to the something I'd like to know. Why did he tell me you'd had a miscarriage?"

In fact, Flynn discovered himself considerably irritated over the question. If he hadn't thought Pride had lost the baby, he probably would have continued searching for her until he found her. Then he wouldn't be in this fix today.

"I really don't know the answer to that," she replied, "but I suspect it had something to do with his dislike of having everybody know his daughter was an unwed mother." Pride kept her gaze focused on her coffee cup. "Once I left Houston, I had no further communication with him."

"Do you happen to know why he told me you were in New York?" Flynn asked, in his calmest voice.

"New York," Pride repeated, in the same tones she would have said, "Outer Mongolia."

"Yes, New York. He said you had a job offer from a major women's magazine, and that you intended to take it."

Pride looked surprised. "Heavens, Flynn, I have no idea. It's true that I had received a good job offer from a New York–based magazine, but I never intended to accept it." She paused, frowning. "I don't think I even told him about the offer. By that time, I wasn't talking to him anymore."

"I see." Flynn kept his voice calm and steady with a great effort, even though he now realized Pride knew nothing about her father's state of mind, or what he had done after her departure.

"If you're trying to lead up to something, you may as well go ahead and tell me what it is, because none of that is important, if you want my opinion," Pride said in tart tones. "What's important is Johnny. We ought to talk about him instead of things Daddy did that have nothing to do with this."

In his opinion, Judge Donovan's actions had a great deal to do with everything. "We will. I promise." Flynn waited a moment while the waitress set out dishes of ice cream and Pride's slice of pumpkin pie. "But I would like to know why he deliberately misled me into looking for you in New York, when you were practically next door in Louisiana."

Pride caught his gaze. "Maybe he didn't want you to find me," she said after a moment of silence. "Although I certainly don't know why not. I would have thought he would help you find me with a shotgun or something." She shook her head. "I'm sorry, Flynn. I honestly don't know why Daddy would do such a thing. Maybe he intended to tell you the truth when you came to his hospital room."

"Maybe," Flynn said in bleak tones. "If he hadn't died, would you have ever told me about Johnny?"

"Yes, in June, one month from now. I was planning a trip to Houston on a matter of business, so I had assembled in advance all the papers I thought you might like to see. It's a good thing, because when we heard about Daddy's death, everything was already ready."

Flynn relaxed slightly. "Thank you. I appreciate that."

"Not that I thought you'd believe me," she added. "I had pictures of Johnny, just in case, and I also intended to visit your parents and show them the photos."

"You didn't plan to bring Johnny?"

"Not on a business trip." She gave him a commiserating smile. "Arranging for a sitter in Houston would have been a big problem, you know. But if your parents reacted as I thought they might, I would have ready-made babysitters for the next trip."

Flynn hoped he would have believed her, or that at least that he might have had the sense to keep his mouth shut. "My parents took one look at him and knew. I'm sure you're wondering what's wrong with me."

"Your parents have the advantage of remembering what you looked like as a child," Pride said, in dismissive tones. "I would have been satisfied if you finally realized Johnny was my child rather than Gloria's."

"You had a bet on with Gloria," Flynn discovered. "I'll probably never live that one down."

Pride chuckled. "Probably not. But I'll tell you this much, Flynn. Johnny is a real chip off the old block, and you're going to have a lot of fun finding that out these next few days."

His heart lightened. "I'm looking forward to it. In the meantime, I'd just like to say, thank you."

Surprised, she looked up from the pumpkin pie she forked to pieces. "For what? Giving you the shock of your life?"

"For having him." He rose to his feet and came to her side. "For bringing him here." He pulled out her chair and lifted her to her feet, then turned her to face him. "For your willingness to share him with me."

Pride started to reply but he wrapped his arms around her and kissed her.

She let him kiss her as long and as deeply as he wanted, maybe because she thought he couldn't get too carried away in a public restaurant. A moment later, put her arms around his neck and kissed him back. To his delight and amazement, she trembled in his arms in the old way.

A moment later, he came back to earth when the clang of a fork against a dinner plate recalled his surroundings to his dazed mind. He lifted his head and watched Pride's thick, dark eyelashes lift slowly. She looked as dazed as he felt, but as he watched, her expression turned to one of stunned dismay.

"It will all work out, darling," he said gently. "You'll see."

He pulled her chair out for her and seated her again.

The moment he did, the restaurant burst into applause.

Pride's face took on the color of a ripe tomato and she refused to look at him. He smiled and waved to the other diners then sat back down.

He should have thought to provide himself with an engagement ring, he thought, watching Pride assume a distant expression.

Not that it would have helped. Even if he got a ring on her finger, she might well have "lost" it in another five minutes.

He needed a plan.

More than that, he needed help, and he thought he knew where to start.

On that thought, Flynn arrived early at his office the next morning. Last night, Pride had finally kissed him with all the passion he remembered, even though she spent the rest of the evening behind a wall of smiling distance.

Fortunately, he'd had the good sense to tell Pride he had no intentions of fighting with her over custody of Johnny. He would take whatever she allowed him in terms of visitation rights and time.

It went sorely against the grain with him, but he knew he had said the right thing for once when Pride relaxed somewhat, gave him a cautious smile and said she had no objections to changing Johnny's last name to Sutherland.

He had made such a mess of things, he would do things right this time if it killed him. At the moment, Flynn rather thought it might, because he wanted to demand everything, including a wedding.

He left his desk, where he had been pouring over the copy of Johnny's birth certificate Pride gave him and stared blindly out the windows at the downtown Houston traffic below. Pride had named him as Johnny's father on the certificate. Moreover, Johnny's name was John Morgan Donovan. She had given Johnny his paternal grandfather's name. The realization almost knocked the breath out of Flynn.

Sounds outside the office door indicated Killeen had arrived. Moments later, a knock sounded on his door and Killeen entered, clutching a folded-open *Houston Chronicle*.

"I just noticed something, boss," she said. "Look at this photo of Tracy Eric. Does it remind you of anyone?"

Killeen laid the newspaper on his desk, and Flynn bent over it. He rubbed his eyes and stared at the photograph of the attractive, dark-headed woman who called herself Tracy Eric.

"Offhand, no." How could she expect him to care about some single-mommy newspaper columnist at a time like this?

Flynn reminded himself that Killeen knew nothing about the events of—had it really been less than twenty-four hours?—yesterday and held onto his temper with both hands. He needed her help, and he did not want her wasting time on the ubiquitous Tracy Eric.

"Look again, boss."

Flynn looked again but still couldn't discern a resemblance to anyone he knew. Rather than snap at Killeen, he let his gaze drift down to the column proper, and he began to read.

Tracy Eric wrote about seeing "him" again, the man who had made her pregnant. Her exploration of her own feelings made Flynn feel as though he were sitting across the table from a woman who was baring her soul.

His attention duly caught, he read on. Tracy Eric had seen the man at her father's funeral. Her detailing of the things she had noticed about the man she had once loved made Flynn think she ought to write novels instead of true-to-life columns.

Tracy now faced the ordeal of telling the man about the son he'd sired. Would he be a good father to her son?

"All single moms face this question, even if our child's father behaves like a father. We ask ourselves, where is he when the tough questions arise? The big decisions? Where is he every darned day, when we're the ones who have to apply the consistent, no-nonsense discipline every child needs?"

Tracy went on to wonder if the man, assuming he accepted his fatherhood, would spoil her son.

"If so," she wrote, *"I'll accept it. Even if I have to be the heavy, the one who says no while his father showers him with expensive gifts and exciting trips, I want my son to know and love his father."*

Flynn nodded. At least the woman had the right attitude. A child needed a father to love and respect, even if the father wasn't good for anything but fluff, as Tracy implied. The child's well-being was all-important to Tracy, and Flynn had to respect her for that view.

Killeen, who had been waiting patiently while he read the column, grinned at him.

"Don't you just love her? She's single-handedly responsible for keeping me from telling my kids what a no-good turkey their father is. I'm telling you, boss, I almost slipped this morning. If I hadn't read that column first thing..."

Flynn chuckled. "Maybe the absentee fathers of the city should vote to award Tracy Eric a medal of some sort."

"She deserves it," Killeen said darkly. "Look again, boss. This woman was in our office yesterday morning."

Flynn thought but couldn't recall any women who had been in his office the morning before, other than Pride and her cousin Gloria.

His eyes widened.

Killeen nodded enthusiastically. "What do you think? It's doesn't look much like her, but it's her all right."

"Gloria Boudreaux?"

Flynn folded the paper into smaller sections and held it closer to his eyes. There was a strong resemblance, now that he thought about it.

"I'm certain it's her," Killeen said. "What put me on to it was the two kids, Tracy and Eric. I thought it was a coincidence at first, until I realized that the first thing a mother would do is name herself after her kids."

"Pride is a freelance writer." Flynn wondered if his brain had turned to mush. "Maybe her cousin has the same talent."

"Tracy Eric only talks about her son, but Gloria Boudreaux has two little girls, as well," Killeen noted.

Flynn recollected another fact. "Gloria Boudreaux is not a single mother. From all I hear, her husband is the type of man who's in on every aspect of his children's upbringing."

Killeen stared at the photograph. "It has to be her. The coincidence is just too much."

Flynn froze. For an entire minute, he stared at the column and said absolutely nothing.

When he became conscious of Killeen's curious stare, he cleared his throat. "I don't think Gloria is Tracy Eric."

Why was Pride Donovan writing a column under the pretext of being a single mother?

Because she was a single mother, his battered brain reminded him.

"Killeen?"

His secretary looked up.

"Those four children in here yesterday. Did you think they were all Gloria Boudreaux's children?"

"Oh, gosh, no." Killeen grinned. "It's fairly obvious that the little blond boy, the one who ate your watch, is Pride Donovan's son."

"Is it obvious?" Flynn asked, in weak tones.

Killeen stared at him. "Are you trying to tell me he isn't her son? Any mother would swear Miss Donovan was that little kid's mother. I mean, the way she looked out for him, and scolded him. I'd swear he was her child."

Flynn wondered if he ought to resign from the legal profession on the grounds of being a mental incompetent.

On the other hand, most lawyers he knew seemed as focused on the wrong things as he now perceived himself to be.

However, nobody said he had to remain stupid.

"You're right," he said. "Johnny is Ms. Donovan's son." He drew in his breath and added, "I'm going to need some help, Ms. Ross. I'm facing the biggest battle of my life, because, you see, Johnny is also my son."

*

Pride awakened early after a mostly sleepless night and stared at the sunlit ceiling. Flynn intended to take her and Johnny to the zoo, after she came by his office finish the work on her inheritance. He had invited the Boudreaux family also, but Gloria flatly refused.

"You and Flynn need to spend some time alone with Johnny," she said. "Johnny needs to experience Flynn in the position of father, and you need to adjust to the idea yourself."

Pride scowled at the window. She figured she had adjusted about as much as she could, and spending time alone with Flynn was a really bad idea. She still harbored some sort of major attraction for Flynn. Who knew what would happen if she allowed herself to be alone with him?

Johnny was a different matter. She'd go along on the trip to the zoo for Johnny's sake, but she wasn't about to marry Flynn just to provide Johnny with two resident parents. She reminded herself that Flynn wanted Johnny very badly, and that complicated matters between them considerably.

Flynn had surprised her with his ready acceptance of fatherhood and with his willingness to let her specify his paternal rights. She intended to bide her time and see if he really meant it. On that thought she fell back to sleep.

She didn't awaken until Johnny tugged at the covers.

"Flowers," he said.

Pride came awake and blinked at her son. Gloria must have already dressed him, she realized. His small face reflected excitement and curiosity.

"Flowers," Johnny repeated. "Flynn."

"Daddy," she corrected automatically. She sat up and rubbed at her eyes. "What's all this about flowers?"

"Johnny, I told you not to wake your mother up," Gloria scolded from the door. "Sorry, Pride. I thought you needed the extra sleep. Now that you're awake, come on out here and smell the roses."

"What roses?"

"You'll see."

Gloria withdrew with such a portentous expression that Pride hastened out of bed and threw on a pale green chenille robe. When she walked into the living room, the white decor was enhanced by splashes of brilliant color all around the room. Lots of brilliant red color, she saw, and it all came from the dozens of roses scattered about on every available surface. Gloria must have put every vase in the house into use and pressed a few water glasses into service also.

"What on earth is this?" Pride stood in the center of the living room, dazed and blinking.

"Someone, who shall remain unnamed since I refuse to snoop in the little cards, is employing flower language to tell you something."

The doorbell sounded.

"Flynn," Johnny shouted and raced toward the door, followed by the three Boudreaux children, who lived in constant expectation of their father's homecoming.

Gloria grinned at Pride and indicated the door. "It's your turn to do the honors. I've been answering it all morning."

"What time is it?" Pride asked, groaning.

"Almost nine."

"Oh, no. I'm supposed to be at Flynn's office by eleven." She headed for the door, where the children bounced up and down.

"Ms. Pride Donovan? Flower delivery. Sign here, please." The delivery man held three long boxes, stacked on top of one another.

Pride signed and received the boxes. Gloria came to the door and peered at the delivery truck as the man walked away.

"That's the fifth different truck that's arrived this morning. He must have cleaned out every red rose in every flower shop in town, because that van is from Winnie."

Pride squinted at the van. Sure enough, its side bore the logo of a flower shop in the nearby town.

"So it is," she said. "What's going on here, anyway?"

"You tell us. Quiet, kids. Aunt Pride can't open it until she gets it to the kitchen table."

Pride opened the box at the kitchen table, with the four excited children and Gloria looking on. As she'd expected, the boxes contained another three dozen red roses.

"What on earth am I supposed to do with all these roses?" Pride wondered what madhouse she'd strayed into.

"We're all out of vases," Gloria said. "I've started on the water glasses, unless you happen to know where some more vases are hidden."

"Just look at these, Gloria. Aren't they beautiful?"

Gloria agreed. "Aren't you going to read the card?"

"We already know who sent them." She opened the small envelope enclosed in the box and read aloud a date. "That was almost two years ago. What on earth do you think it means?"

She opened the five other cards Gloria brought her. Each one bore the same date, but no signature.

Gloria shrugged and shook her head. "You were staying with us then, and Johnny was only a few weeks old, so it can't be an anniversary between the two of you. Can you recall anything important from that period of time?"

"Other than my miserable battle to breastfeed Johnny? At that time, I was one of the living dead, so my memory isn't the best."

"Think about it," Gloria said. "In the meantime, Flynn awaits."

"Oh, no." Pride raced for the shower.

She thought on the date during the drive to Houston. Beside her, Johnny chattered about the upcoming delights at the zoo, and Pride wondered what on earth she missed. That date must commemorate something.

She still hadn't remembered anything when she pushed open the door to Flynn's office and smiled at Killeen Ross, who grinned back. Her portentous expression reminded Pride of Gloria's expression earlier that morning.

"Come in, Miss Donovan," Killeen said. "He's expecting you. Go right on in. Hello, young man. I hear you're going to the zoo this afternoon."

"Zoo," Johnny agreed. "Monkeys. Tigers."

"That's right. You can tell me all about it when you get back." Killeen stood and opened the door for Pride to pass into the office.

Pride stepped inside and wondered if she'd come to the right place. Six trays of diamond rings, mixed with emeralds, sapphires, and pearls, sat on Flynn's desk. The jewels caught the light and reflected it back in rainbows of sparkling, shimmering color.

"Pretty," Johnny exclaimed and struggled to get to the desk.

"Come in, Pride." Flynn stepped forward to take Johnny from her arms. "Step right up and take your pick."

Pride stared at him, even as she noticed the three other men in the room, two wearing the uniforms of various security firms. Flynn wore a tan jacket over a plaid shirt and a pair of khaki trousers, which seemed incongruous among all the uniforms and the dark suit of the third man, who regarded the jewels in a proprietary fashion.

"What?" she asked, in blank astonishment.

"I'm showering you with diamonds," Flynn said in grave tones. "You get to pick and choose the one, or ones, you want."

"Showering me with—"

She broke off, eyes widening. At last she recalled the significance of the date and the roses. On that date, she had struggled to breastfeed a colicky baby who cried all night, while writing a weekly "Single Mommy" column. She'd been so exhausted and so frustrated that she tackled the subject of what she'd do if her ex-lover suddenly appeared on her doorstep, wanting her to take him back.

Pride turned to stare at Flynn. She wrote that first, before she would so much as listen to him, he would have to shower her with roses and diamonds. Then he'd have to beg her on bended knee, in the proper fashion, to give him another chance.

Of course, the column had been tongue-in-cheek, and her readers understood that, although they agreed wholeheartedly with the sentiments expressed. But Flynn couldn't possibly have been reading Tracy Eric all this time... could he? He didn't even know she wrote the Tracy Eric column.

She sighed. Killeen read the column faithfully, and she might have showed Flynn a column that contained something Flynn would recognize. Flynn had probably recognized her writing style.

Obviously, he had done some fast reading. She glanced at him. He kissed Johnny's cheek while his brown eyes followed her.

"If you dare try the bended-knee bit on me, Flynn Sutherland," she said, "I won't be responsible for my actions."

Flynn bounced Johnny in his arms to keep him from leaping onto the trays of sparkling diamonds and laughed.

"Hush up and choose, Pride," he said. "Or does showering you with diamonds mean you want all of them?"

"Neither. Send them back."

"Not until you choose something. Get over here, woman. These men are busy."

Pride glanced at the three men. All three hid smiles.

"They're enjoying the break from routine," she said. "It isn't every day they get to see a woman brain a man with a sheaf of roses and a tray of diamonds."

"Flynn's," Johnny squealed and pounced on Flynn's wrist.

Flynn caught the child and tucked him under one arm while he removed his mariner's watch. "Sorry. I forgot about my watch. You guys didn't happen to bring a selection of watches, did you?"

Johnny registered a loud complaint about Flynn's bare wrist and twisted to eye the trays on Flynn's desk with lustful brown eyes.

Under the cover of this by-play, Pride advanced on the desk and bent over the trays. Who wouldn't be fascinated by the display of multi-colored, sparkling gems? She found them all spectacular.

"Try this one," Flynn tapped a glittering emerald.

Pride couldn't resist. She took out the emerald and slipped it on her finger.

"Wrong hand," Flynn said. "It goes on the left hand."

"It's too big." Pride removed the ring, surprised at her own reluctance to part with it.

"It can be sized. Do you like it?"

"Like it? Who wouldn't like it?"

She studied the tray and selected another ring like a person in a dream then tried on several more rings. She reached for the emerald again. The square-cut stone surrounded by diamonds sparked with shafts of multi-colored light, yet didn't overwhelm her hand. She loved it.

"I thought so." Flynn looked satisfied. "With your eyes, emeralds are perfect."

"Jewels like these don't go properly with my outfit."

She wore a pair of dark blue slacks and a middy blouse, probably in honor of Flynn's nautical leanings. Emeralds called for a slinky white dress. A dress, period.

"We'll take this one." Flynn held up the emerald. "Size it to this size." He held out another ring that had fit her third finger perfectly.

"Flynn, I forbid you to buy that ring," Pride said.

"Hush, Pride. You don't want to air our dirty linen in public, do you?" He dropped both rings into one of the suited man's hands.

The man slipped the two rings into an envelope and stowed it inside his jacket. Then the men packed all the trays into a box and left the office.

"Flynn, don't you dare buy that ring."

"I'm fulfilling all your conditions," Flynn said. "Therefore, you have to listen and come back to me."

"That was journalism," Pride informed him. "Tracy Eric has her act together. Pride is still in a state of uproar."

"So is your 'ex-lover,'" Flynn said. "For your information, as far as I'm concerned, I'm still your lover."

Pride blinked at him, still bemused by the trays of diamonds and Flynn's evident intention of buying her a ring, whether she accepted it or not.

"Have you been involved with anyone since you left Houston three years ago?" he asked.

"No, I have not." Pride frowned at him. "As you can see, I haven't had time." She indicated Johnny.

Flynn set Johnny's small feet on the thick carpet, and Johnny took off at once for a colorful globe that sat on a stand in the corner of the room.

"Sit down, Pride. Before you sign the papers concerning your father's property, I'd like to talk to you a moment about us."

"There is no us," Pride insisted, but she followed Flynn to the sofa where she'd sat with Gloria and the children only two days ago.

"There is still quite a lot between us, whether you want to admit it or not." Flynn sat down beside her.

Pride watched Johnny spin the globe while she reminded herself that Johnny was the only thing between them now.

"I want to be a father to my son," Flynn said. "I want to be with him as much as I can."

Pride respected that. "You might as well know I'm thinking about moving back to Houston. Most of my contacts are here, and the freelance market is definitely bigger—"

"That isn't what I meant. I want to live in the same house with Johnny. I want to help you put him to bed at night, and hear his prayers, and teach him to pitch a baseball."

"You'll have plenty of opportunity for all those things."

"Not if I live a mile or two across town from him. Pride—"

"I'm not ready to discuss this any further today, Flynn." She doubted she'd ever be ready to discuss it. "Johnny's going to get impatient before long."

Flynn made a sound of frustration. "We had something good together, once. As far as I'm concerned, we still do. Don't you think we could have something even better if we both tried?"

She closed her eyes and turned her face away. "I don't know, Flynn. Sexual attraction is very different from what's needed to make a successful marriage, if that's what you have in mind."

"You know very well it is." Flynn smiled at her. "Are you saying you still feel sexually attracted to me? Well, that's something."

Confused, Pride flushed and kept her face turned away. It was harder than she'd dreamed to sit beside the man she still loved with all her heart and pretend she felt only bare hints of the powerful physical and emotional attraction that she once hadn't bothered to hide.

Because he still attracted her in all the old ways, and in a new and even more meaningful way. It had to do with how he looked at Johnny, she realized. Flynn wanted them to be a family. She considered it a step in the right direction.

Or the wrong direction if there remained no love between them. She had to be very careful, or she would find herself in the same situation as her mother.

She saw Flynn watching her and swallowed hard.

He took her hand and rose, pulling her up with him. "Let's take our son to the zoo before he figures out how to take that globe apart and eat it."

Chapter Nine

Johnny had a ball at the zoo. Pride walked beside Flynn and kept a close eye on Johnny as he toddled ahead of them on the walks. She noted the way Flynn kept his hand at her waist in his old, protective manner. The very warmth of his hand sent a thrill over her entire body.

Later, they sat together on a bench beneath a tree and rested. Johnny climbed into Flynn's lap and laid his head on Flynn's chest. Flynn draped his other arm over the back of the bench behind Pride and stretched out his legs.

"Enjoying yourself?" he asked.

"I'm having a wonderful time," Pride said in all honesty.

"It could be like this all the time." After a moment, he indicated the child's head beneath his chin. "Did you breastfeed Johnny?"

Pride cast her mind back frantically to the Tracy Eric columns from that era of her life. Yes, there had been one on breastfeeding. It had been a doozey, thanks to her experiences during that time.

"Why don't you read Tracy Eric and find out?" she asked.

"I have, thank you. Tracy Eric has a way of drawing together both her experiences and other people's. I'm interested in your experience—what really happened. Once you get going on paper, something else takes over."

"Are you saying I get possessed by an evil spirit?" she teased, lifting her brows.

Flynn chuckled and kissed Johnny's forehead. "Actually, the Pride who writes intimidates me. I can't sift through your deathless prose and distinguish between what you really felt at the time and the relationships you saw days later, after you had time to think about it and pull everything together."

Pride quivered with pleasure. Then she caught herself. Flynn could easily seduce her with appreciation—the praise she had never gotten from her father.

"The relationships are the reason editors buy my stuff," she pointed out.

"Well, I'm not an editor. All I want is honest answers to my questions. I have three years of your life and two of Johnny's to catch up on."

"It wasn't very interesting," Pride muttered. "I wrote and Johnny grew."

"Your column on the womanly art of breastfeeding gave me a whole, new concept of child-rearing. Did you succeed?"

"I tried."

"What does that mean?"

"It means I couldn't. I didn't produce enough milk, and Johnny fretted constantly until I started supplementing the breastfeedings with a bottle."

"You must have been exhausted." Flynn studied her.

She kept her gaze forward and made no comment. That particular era of her life wasn't one she cared to remember.

"It must have been rough," he observed. "Trying to earn a living and care for a colicky baby by yourself—"

"I wasn't by myself," she interjected. "I had the benefit of Gloria's experience."

"I wish you had called me then. What you probably needed was rest and care." Flynn touched her face with his fingertips. "Pride..."

"Better change the subject, Flynn. You're in over your head when it comes to the womanly art of breastfeeding."

"I've been in over my head ever since I saw you again." He smiled. "You were exhausted, weren't you?"

She might as well tell him. "Yes, I was, if you want to know. Johnny cried all night for weeks, and I was at my wits' end. If it hadn't been for Gloria telling me to quit listening to the doctor and start bottle-feeding the baby, I'd have probably gone berserk."

Flynn thought on this a moment. "Are you saying Johnny was crying because he wasn't getting enough to eat?"

"That's the logical conclusion." Pride pinpointed a male cardinal in the tree over their heads and focused all her attention on it. "At any rate, the day I listened to Gloria, I had the first uninterrupted night's sleep I'd had in a long time. It was wonderful."

Flynn stared at her. Cradling Johnny in one arm, he drew Pride closer with the other and kissed her temple.

"Those days are over," he said. "From now on, I'll always be there to help you."

The words were a vow, and Pride registered them in her heart as well as her mind, even while she reminded herself that vows were often made to be broken.

People passed by in a constant stream. One older couple paused to smile on them and to admire the sleepy little boy lying across Flynn's chest.

"What a lovely child," the elderly woman said. "He looks exactly like his daddy."

Flynn gave her a proud smile. "I think so."

"It's nice to see a young married couple still in love these days," the man said. "Young people nowadays don't know the meaning of commitment. In my day, you didn't have children unless you intended to stay together to raise them."

Flynn agreed in a serious manner.

"Don't let that precious little boy grow up without two parents," the woman warned.

The old couple walked on, and Flynn turned to Pride.

"He won't grow up without two parents who love him," Pride said before he could speak.

He touched her cheek and stroked her tawny hair back from her face. "The way I figure it, I still love you, and I want you to love me. We need to spend time together, the way we did when we first met, so you can get to know me again. What do you say?"

"Isn't that what we've been doing?"

"I'd like to make it official," Flynn said.

Pride nodded with equal gravity. "In that case, you may ask me out tonight. I'll think it over and see if what you suggest sounds good to me."

"Pride."

"Yes, Flynn?"

"You don't get to think it over. You have to say yes."

"That takes all the fun out of it." She grinned at him. "It's obvious you've been reading Tracy Eric. When did you guess that I was Tracy?"

"I have a super-efficient secretary who's Tracy's Number One fan. She recognized Gloria's picture. Said the kids' names put her on to it."

Pride began to laugh. "Gloria and I thought that picture looked nothing like her, and for obvious reasons, I didn't want to do the column under my own name or photo. Please don't send out any more roses. We've used up every vase and drinking glass in the house, not to mention a few pots and pans."

Flynn chuckled with her. "If you want to be showered with roses and diamonds, then I have to admit, you deserve them."

"A year-and-three-quarters ago, when I wrote that column, I'd have agreed with you," she said in dry tones. "Now that Johnny is a well-adjusted two-year-old who sleeps through the night, I'm a little more reasonable."

"Good." Flynn smoothed Johnny's hair. "Does that mean I can get away with begging you to take me back while sitting on this bench rather than kneeling on the ground?"

*

Pride arrived home with Johnny and discovered the Boudreaux family packing up to return to Lake Charles. She had known Gloria would be returning home today, because Eddie was due in early the following morning.

"Maybe we can stay on another day," Gloria suggested, studying Pride.

"I wouldn't let you. A man has a right to the peace and comfort of his own family when he's been two weeks on an off-shore rig."

Gloria, her arms full of paper sacks containing children's clothing, plopped down on the white sofa beside Pride, who had taken a moment out to tie Johnny's shoe laces.

"What are you going to do about Flynn?" she asked. "How do you feel about him, now that you've had time to be with him again? And I don't mean that fatherhood stuff you write about as Tracy Eric."

Pride shoved back a lock of her tawny hair and kept her gaze on Johnny's shoes. "I... still have feelings for him."

"Are we talking man–woman type feelings here, or are we talking the same kind of romantic trivia you wrote about in your last column?"

Pride gulped. She wrote that column before she realized Flynn knew about Tracy Eric, and Flynn had been thrilled with it when it appeared. It had taken careful note of the leap of Tracy's heart upon beholding her former lover once more.

Gloria, however, looked at things more seriously.

"I didn't know you thought romantic feelings were trivia," Pride said, grinning. "This, from one of the two people who makes Vesuvius look like a worn-out toaster?"

"Get real. Of course Eddie and I are all-out romantics. What I'm talking about here is grown-up stuff, like forbearance and forgiveness. Without them, no marriage can survive for long."

Pride kept her attention on Johnny as she set his feet on the floor. He scampered toward the kitchen, where the other children were eating breakfast.

"You'll have to forgive Flynn for the way he hurt you three years ago," Gloria pointed out, "and overlook the fact that he wasn't there for you when Johnny was born."

Pride mulled it over. "I'll have to explore the matter in an upcoming column."

"You're hopeless." Gloria sprang up. "If you want to know what I think, Pride Donovan, it's that you write that column to avoid the feelings you want to avoid. No one, including you, wants to hear about forgiveness."

Pride nodded. "I think you're right."

"While you're at it, you can forgive your father."

"I already have."

"Not in your heart. You think you've got it all neatly pigeon-holed in your brain, but you haven't forgiven him any more than you've forgiven Flynn. Before you can trust yourself to Flynn or any other man, you're going to have to sort all those things out and realize you are not your mother."

"I'll start on a column tonight," Pride promised.

"I'll never understand writers." Gloria picked up the sacks to carry out to her SUV. "But I do know one thing. The reason your column is so popular is because all the other single moms out there are full of the same feelings of betrayal and hurt as you are."

"The column is popular for a reason," Pride agreed.

Gloria leaned forward. "Until you overcome your past, you'll never be happy. Just like lots of those other single mothers will never be happy. It's too much fun to hold onto all the hurt and bitterness."

Pride chuckled. "What we need here is a marriage guidance column by the most happily married woman in Louisiana and most of Texas, Mrs. Gloria Boudreaux."

"Only I'll call myself Sylvia John," Gloria returned, and headed toward the front door. "Think about it, Pride. If you want to know my opinion, it's that you're holding on to your anger at Flynn in order to cover up your own guilt over not telling him two years ago about Johnny."

Pride frowned. "I told Flynn I was pregnant three years ago. And told him and told him. Why should I feel guilty?"

"Because you're letting your father's actions poison your future," Gloria replied. "Can't you see that the poor man made himself three times as miserable as he ever made you?"

Pride watched Gloria shove open the door with her armload of sacks. She got to her feet and went to the bedroom to gather up another armload of Gloria's sacks. She knew her father had been a miserably unhappy man. Maybe Gloria was right about him.

But Gloria was all wrong about her motives. She was merely being cautious, and who could blame her?

"I don't feel guilty in the least," she said. "It wasn't my fault Flynn chose not to believe me."

"You've convicted Flynn of being just like your father, and all because he really believed he couldn't have children." Gloria set the sacks in the rear of her SUV and regarded Pride. "One thing is obvious. Flynn wants you, and he wants Johnny. You're going to have to make a decision." She grinned suddenly. "Maybe with me and the kids out of the house, you'll have enough peace and quiet to do a little straight thinking for once."

With Gloria and her three children gone, Pride had so much opportunity to think, it almost drove her crazy. She wrote the beginning of a column that skimmed the surface of her feelings. The activity left her regarding the deeper emotions with trepidation. She wound up shoving all her doubts into the back of her mind to be dealt with later, probably in an upcoming Tracy Eric column. Tracy Eric, unlike Pride Donovan, never acted until she had digested and reformulated all the facts.

A day later, after spending the afternoon with Flynn and Johnny at a Houston Astros baseball game, Pride suddenly realized that Flynn treated her the way he once had, with the tender, teasing affection that once turned her bones to water.

That thought led to a consideration of whether or not he still harbored anger at her for not telling him about Johnny. If he did, she detected absolutely no sign of it.

She stirred chili in a saucepan over the stove in Flynn's apartment and tried not to look conscious of his steady regard.

"You enjoy cooking, don't you?" Flynn asked.

Tracy Eric had done a column or two on childhood nutrition. Flynn had made no secret of the fact that he'd read and studied every single one of Tracy Eric's columns.

"It's a lot of fun, if you approach it right," she said. "Cooking in a bachelor's kitchen is definitely a challenge."

"Come on, Pride. I stocked this kitchen with you and Johnny in mind. What I meant was, you really enjoy making a home for Johnny."

Pride smiled at him. "I suppose I do. I've been very lucky. Being a writer has enabled me to be at home with him a lot more than a nine-to-five job would have."

"And it let you experience being a single working mother enough to write the Tracy Eric column," he agreed. "Where do writers get their ideas, I wonder? Am I going to read about my efforts at parenting in an upcoming column?"

Pride shook her head and laughed. "Although, now that you mention it, Tracy Eric could do a lot with your approach to fatherhood."

Flynn brightened. "She could? Do you think she approves of my approach?"

"Of course she does." She couldn't resist the hopeful expression on his face. Anyone would approve of the way Flynn had overcome his shock and had done his best to be a father to Johnny. "Tracy Eric thinks Johnny is a lucky little boy."

"Me," Johnny yelled from his comfortable position on Flynn's lap.

"Yes, that's you, young man. And while we're on the subject of lucky, you and I need to have a little talk about how you're supposed to behave when you're visiting Daddy's house."

Johnny flung his arms around Flynn's neck. "Daddy's house."

"That's right." Pride tapped her spoon on the pan for emphasis. "When you're visiting Daddy's house, you don't run through the living room with a glass of milk in your hand. You don't run, period." She regarded her son. "You don't want Daddy changing his mind about his luck in having you, do you?"

"Now, Pride, what's a glass of milk on the carpet?" Flynn asked, grinning.

"There's a principle involved here, and it has nothing to do with the work involved in cleaning the carpet."

"Even when you did the all work?" Flynn asked in meek tones.

"Careful, Flynn, or I'll have a little talk with you in addition to the one I'm about to have with Johnny."

"Uh-oh. Daddy needs to child-proof his apartment," Flynn said, cuddling Johnny.

"True," Pride said. "Just like you had to child-proof your wrist."

Flynn glanced at the plain, Timex watch he'd bought to tide him over Johnny's fascination with mariner's watches and laughed. Johnny had accorded the watch serious study but abandoned it in favor of something more colorful.

"The truth is, I haven't the faintest idea how to go about child-proofing," Flynn admitted. "Maybe you could help me out."

"Tonight," she promised.

Since Johnny had already done some damage to Flynn's apartment, and Pride had spotted several other hazardous items Johnny would surely investigate, she figured she'd better help Flynn immediately after supper.

She served bowls of chili and a green salad, and both males appeared well-satisfied. In fact, the satisfaction on Flynn's face served to make her blush.

"Johnny has had a busy day," Flynn observed when the little boy began nodding off after the meal.

"I'm not surprised. Let's put him down on the sofa, and I'll show you the basics of child-proofing."

"Better put a pillow alongside him." Flynn lifted the sleepy child and laid him gently on the sofa. "We don't want him rolling off."

She followed him to his bedroom, glancing in a guarded way around Flynn's bedroom while he took a pillow from the bed. The bedroom was the only room in the small apartment that had character, chiefly because Flynn had set framed photographs on every available surface.

Pride jerked her gaze away from the bedside table. It wouldn't do to let Flynn know she searched the photographs for evidence of other women in his life.

"Those are of you." He pointed to a group of small frames.

The smile on his face set the seal to her irritation and she flushed. "Really? Why on earth would you keep photos of me in the middle of this harem?"

"The rest are of my parents and my relatives." Flynn kissed Johnny's forehead. "Take a look."

Pride ignored the invitation. "I'll have to send you some of Johnny. I have a beautiful picture of him in bed with his teddy."

"Kiss our son goodnight," Flynn ordered. "I want to talk to you."

What on earth had she said? Pride tucked the pillow alongside the little boy then backed off as Flynn turned off all the lights in the room except one small lamp on the opposite side of the room.

"In here." He looked grim as he held the door open for her to precede him into the bedroom.

Too late, she realized being in a bedroom alone with Flynn was a bad idea.

"All right, Pride," he said. "I just want to know one thing.

Have you included me, along with your father, on your list of unforgivable people?"

Her hand jerked in his, and she tried to withdraw it. "Heavens, Flynn, what a question. I don't have a list of unforgivable people, and if I did, neither you nor my father, would be on it."

"Is that so?" Flynn pulled her down to sit beside him on the edge of the bed. "You could have fooled me. That disinterested act of yours always makes me wonder if you even know my name."

"I don't know what you mean."

"Yes, you do. You were looking almost human a little earlier, until I told you to have a look around."

Pride lowered her gaze to keep him from seeing that her eyes had filled with tears. "I'm sorry, Flynn. Of course I forgive you." She forced a smile. "If you're interested, I forgave you the day you rescued Johnny from the water."

She lifted her gaze to meet his for a brief instant. He regarded her sternly, and straightened to hold her in place by clasping her shoulders.

"Why don't I believe you?" he asked.

"I'm sure I don't know." She looked away. "I learned years ago how to look as if I didn't care about things my father would say when he tried to hurt me or my mother."

"I know Johnny is my son. It's my own fault that I've missed out on two years of my son's life, and three years I could have spent with you. Can't you let that rank as sufficient suffering to redeem me in your eyes?"

"You're mistaken if you think I want you to suffer," Pride said. "Since there isn't any proof I can offer you, you'll have to take my word for it that I forgive you for not believing me three years ago."

Flynn searched her face. Whatever he saw there seemed to satisfy him. "There is some proof you can offer me."

"What is it?"

"You can kiss me."

"What will that prove, other than the fact that I find you sexually attractive?"

Flynn smiled, a sudden expression of pure joy that wiped the severe look from his face. "Do you find me sexually attractive?"

Pride felt heat rising in her cheeks once more and refused to meet his gaze. "I slept with you, didn't I? The proof of that is lying in the middle of your sofa at the moment."

"That was then. This is now." He drew her inexorably closer. "I need some current proof. I need to know you've forgiven me. I need to know if you still feel anything at all for me." He closed the small distance between their bodies. "I need you, Pride. Please kiss me."

If he'd tried to force her, Pride could have resisted, but she had no defense against the humble plea. She closed her eyes and let him turn her chin up.

"Pride," he whispered.

She opened her eyes.

"That's better," he said and kissed her.

The warm pressure of his lips on hers made her tremble. His hand at the small of her back brought her closer still, and his brown eyes looked into hers as he touched his lips gently to hers.

She parted her lips, sensing his desire, and he accepted the unspoken invitation. His tongue invaded her mouth, and she sighed her pleasure.

It felt wonderful to kiss Flynn, knowing that there were no more secrets between them. She closed her eyes, moaning softly as he deepened the pressure of the kiss.

"Pride, you feel so good," he said, at last. "You go straight to my head, just the way you always did."

She could say the same thing. Inhaling Flynn's favorite citrus cologne and feeling the brush of his hair on her forehead made her senses spin. The warm pressure of his body against hers finished her off, and Pride went down without a fight.

"Am I proving anything?" she asked, her voice a throaty murmur.

"Other than the fact that you're driving me insane?" His faint laughter sounded choked. "You make me want to go crazy."

He ran his hands over her body, and the slight tremor in them enchanted her.

"Yes," she said, smiling. "But am I proving anything?"

His brown gaze sharpened. "I'll let you know. Do you think you could kiss me again?"

She closed her eyes once more and locked her arms around his neck. Flynn answered her by crushing her against him and kissing her fiercely. His tongue thrust into her mouth with a desperation that encouraged her to slant her face to give him better access. She ran her fingers into his hair and locked him into place.

Flynn kissed her again and again, and Pride encouraged him in every way she knew. His masculine feel and smell made her feel wild and wanton. Being with him constantly these past days reactivated every nerve ending in her body that had ever responded to Flynn Sutherland.

"When you make those little moaning sounds, I want to take you straight to bed," Flynn muttered.

Pride welcomed the idea. She pulled his face back down to hers.

"Pride, stop," he said. "Don't, darling. I want you too badly. If I kiss you again, I won't be able to stop."

Would it be so terrible to make love with Flynn again? Pride thought not. Perhaps she'd even get pregnant again. She kissed him again.

"Pride, will you marry me?"

Flynn shifted her in his arms so that she could put her arms around him and feel the powerful muscles of his back and arms. Pride took full advantage of the opportunity.

"You see?" Flynn said. "I want you more than ever, and I'm

no longer stupid enough to waste time while I figure out how to remind you that I can't have children."

Pride tensed. "You aren't sterile, Flynn."

"If I have problems with the concept of sterility," Flynn said, "don't you think it's possible you have problems with the concept of trust? You were right when you said the real definition of my condition was a low sperm count," Flynn said in gentle tones. "Dad was so hung up on the idea of grandchildren, he defined it as sterility." He ran his hand over the back of her head. "It'll be a while before I get accustomed to thinking of myself as a reasonably fertile male."

She smiled. "I told you, a lot depends on finding a truly compatible woman."

She found it hard to remember that Flynn might start mistrusting Johnny's parentage when he held her like this.

"That's you," Flynn said.

While in his arms, Pride knew he was right. She felt the warm pressure of his lips on hers and sighed with pleasure. He rocked his lips against hers, until she parted for him, then his tongue entered her mouth and stroked her tongue gently.

She shivered with delight and explored his mouth in the same way he explored hers. His arms tightened around her until she almost had trouble breathing, and she enjoyed the feeling thoroughly.

His skin grew heated beneath the cotton shirt, and Pride ran her hands over the hard muscles of his shoulders and arms, savoring the heat of him beneath her palms. If possible, the muscles grew even harder as she stroked lightly over them. The scent of his favorite citrus aftershave tantalized her further.

"Touch me," he whispered and waited while her fumbling fingers struggled with the buttons of his shirt.

Pride tossed the shirt aside at last, and he fairly ripped his undershirt off. She ran her fingers into his hair covering his chest, stroking her palms over his pectoral muscles.

Flynn groaned his pleasure in her explorations and encouraged her to explore him further. He drove his tongue into her mouth with greater urgency.

Pride answered his desire and locked her arms around his neck. He molded her against his body, and she felt the heat his skin gave off increase as her skin contacted his. Before she knew it, he'd pulled her T-shirt off over her head, and her bare breasts were flattened against his chest.

An astounding thing happened. One moment, she was enjoying the pleasant, physical contact with his strong, male body, and the next moment she wanted to force him down on the bed so she could ravish him.

Pride reversed the kiss. Where he had been kissing her, now she kissed him. She unlocked her arms from around his neck and used her hands to explore his body, until he was gasping with pleasure as she forced him to yield to her wishes.

Flynn had no reserves about yielding to a woman. He let her force him to lie beside her on the bed so she could kiss his chest and taste him to her heart's content. When her tongue flicked over his nipple, his body jerked and he groaned.

His fingers gripped her shoulders. She felt the cool air on her bare breasts before she realized he had lifted her to expose her to his enraptured gaze. An instant later, he reversed their positions yet again.

He hovered over her, arching her body up to his mouth. He closed his lips over one breast and drew warmly at it.

The fierce pleasure electrified her. Moaning, she dug her fingernails into his shoulders and lifted toward him.

"Pride, you're so beautiful," he murmured. "I want you more than ever. Will you marry me?"

Her eyes flew open. His tanned face was taut with desire, and his brown eyes glowed with emotion. His mouth hovered over her breast, as if tantalizing her with pleasures to come if she said yes.

She drew in an audible breath, unable to speak.

Flynn lowered his head and took her into his mouth again. She flung back her head as the warm drawing started a shivery desire in the pit of her stomach.

"We can have more children," he whispered against her skin.

Pride groaned, realizing that event could be more imminent than she thought. Flynn's warm tongue flicked across her bare breast, his breath tickled her skin and his hands tormented her with their gentle massage of her waist and buttocks.

She lifted toward him, almost sobbing her desire. She'd think later. Her body had succeeded in shutting her mind down entirely.

"Say yes," Flynn commanded, kissing her neck while his fingers teased her breasts. "Don't you think it's time you put me out of my misery?"

"Stop talking," she said, and fumbled with the buttons on his trousers.

His mouth covered hers. This time, his kiss was an expression of his desire for her, as well as his hope in their future and his longing to give to her.

And to her great relief, he replaced his words with action.

Chapter Ten

Pride awakened in Flynn's arms and lay unmoving while she tried frantically to orient herself. For a moment, she had no idea where she was, until Flynn's tanned shoulder came into focus.

Flynn lay on his side with one arm across her waist as if to make sure she couldn't leave without his knowledge and slept soundly. She listened to his rhythmic breathing for a moment while she scanned as much of her surroundings as she could see without moving and possibly disturbing him.

By raising her head off the pillow just the tiniest bit, she could see his bedside clock. Eight o'clock, she realized with vast relief. She hadn't slept long, and if she was very, very lucky, Johnny still slept soundly on the sofa.

She listened but heard nothing. She considered that a good sign. If Johnny awakened and found himself alone, he would probably go in search of her.

On the other hand, if Johnny went searching and found something interesting, he might abandon his search for his mother in favor of getting into trouble with whatever he had found.

No one could say she didn't know her duty. "Flynn?"

He stirred and opened his eyes. "Is it morning?"

"It's eight o'clock at night, and there's hopefully a little boy still asleep on your sofa."

Flynn stretched and yawned then pulled her closer. "What do you mean hopefully? Didn't you say he sleeps the night through now?" He investigated her neck with his lips.

"If he wakes up, he won't know where he is." Pride struggled to sit up. "He'll go looking for someone."

"In that case, he'll find us right here." He used his arm across her middle to hold her in place.

Pride reminded herself that Flynn had yet to learn what happened when Johnny went looking for anything. "This is your son we're talking about. What do you think will happen if, on his search for us, he happens upon something interesting to eat or take apart?"

He froze a moment then sat up. "Okay. What do we do now?"

"You let me get up to go check on him." Pride sat up. Flynn had turned off the lights, but she could see well enough in the darkened room to find her shirt where he had tossed it on the floor. A moment later, he draped his robe around her shoulders.

"Don't get dressed," he said. "If he's still asleep, you're coming back to bed."

Pride said nothing. Her brain dashed around in search of a reason to leave and came up with nothing. Was she really thinking about spending the night with Flynn? Looking forward to it?

She was, especially if Johnny still slept deeply on the sofa, because then she could excuse her actions by saying Johnny needed to experience spending the night with his father.

Johnny slept as soundly as she hoped, thanks to his busy day. When she turned to go back to the bedroom, Flynn stood in the door watching her and wearing only his trousers.

Pride halted and looked back at him in grave silence. In the dim lighting, his tanned skin glowed golden and his sun-bleached hair framed his face like a halo.

"You look like Apollo," she said and took a step toward him.

He held out a hand to her. "And you must be a sea nymph. You aren't going to vanish on me, are you?"

"Is that what usually happens with sea nymphs?" She walked toward him slowly and put her hand in his.

"Sometimes." He pulled her into the bedroom and closed the door once more. "But I'm hoping the nymph decides to stay with me this time."

He had apparently divined that asking her to marry him made her uncomfortable, so he changed his tactics. Pride stepped into his embrace and rested her face against his chest. So long as Flynn accepted her boundaries, she told herself, she might as well enjoy herself with him. After all, the chances that she would get pregnant again must be almost nil.

In all the time they had spent together three years ago, Flynn had always used protection. Now, she noted as he skimmed his robe off her shoulders and lifted her in his arms, he no longer made the effort.

Maybe he thought Johnny needed a little brother or sister.

On the other hand, maybe he still doubted that Johnny was his, in spite of all the evidence.

"What is it, Pride?" He halted in the middle of the bedroom, with her in his arms.

She opened her eyes, startled. "What do you mean?"

"Something is wrong." He carried her to the bed and sat down, still holding her. "What is it?"

"I just realized that you're no longer taking precautions the way you used to," she said. "Why not?"

He reached over to switch on the bedside lamp. "Because you're the right, compatible woman for me, and I want more children with you."

Well, that answered her question and left her without another word to say.

He placed her carefully on the bed and worked her shirt off over her head. "I want to look at you. Do you mind?"

"Only if I can look at you." Looking at Flynn was sheer pleasure. "Just in case nobody ever told you, having a baby changes a woman's body and not necessarily for the better."

"I don't know about that." Flynn's brown gaze traveled slowly over her breasts with rapt attention. "You're still the most beautiful woman I've ever seen."

She started to question that but thought better of it. If he wanted to say she was beautiful, who was she to argue, so long as she bore in mind the fact that Flynn wanted very badly to marry her, for Johnny's sake.

He laid one hand on her stomach and stroked it over her skin, tracing all the evidences of Johnny's advent.

In answer, she slid her fingers through the hair on his chest then tested the strength of the muscles in his arms and shoulders by probing and kneading them gently.

He leaned over her, studying her body slowly and with grave attention to detail before bending his head to kiss her and trace his tongue over the outline of her lips.

Pride returned the kiss and breathed in the heated scent of his skin with joy and gratitude. No matter what happened between them in the future, at least she had this night to remember, a night when she was almost able to feel as if Flynn loved her again the way he had before she became pregnant with Johnny.

*

Flynn lay beside Pride in the heated aftermath of their lovemaking and wondered what he had done wrong. Making love to Pride affected him as much as ever, but he saw the caution settle over her like a blanket the moment they satisfied their passion.

Sure enough, she still refused to marry him, and he had no idea what he could say to win her consent.

He needed more time with her. Maybe he could wear her down.

"You don't have to go back to Lake Charles," he said. "If you don't want to stay in Anahuac, you can stay here with me."

Pride yawned and snuggled her face against his side. "Johnny and I would be very much in your way if we stayed here. It would be better if we went back to Anahuac." She yawned again and added, "I had planned on staying there another two weeks at least, while I went through everything and got the house ready to sell."

"Why don't we look around at houses?" he suggested. "If you're thinking of moving back to Houston, you'll want a house with a yard for Johnny to play in."

He knew several real estate experts, but on further reflection, he thought his mother might be the better person to help in that direction. She had studied real estate and had a sixth sense about houses.

"I was thinking more in terms of an apartment with a swimming pool and children's play area," she replied. "Houses have yards that have to be kept up."

Flynn noted that she planned to live with Johnny as a single mother in an apartment and not in a house with a yard and a husband. That meant she still did not trust his motives, even though she was willing to make love with him.

He kept a tight grip on himself. Scolding Pride and threatening to haul her off to a justice of the peace most likely would result in her instant flight back to Lake Charles.

"Don't worry about the yard," he said, when he thought he had regained sufficient control of the urge to argue with her. "That's why they invented lawn services."

Pride remained silent, and Flynn resolved to call his mother right away. He needed to present Pride with a house she would find impossible to turn down.

Waking up next to Pride ranked as a major attraction in itself. Too bad, Flynn thought, Pride didn't seem to look at it that way, especially when Johnny awakened early and came in the room to stand beside the bed.

"Good morning, Johnny," he said, when he opened his eyes to find Johnny's little face barely six inches from his. "Do you usually wake up this early?"

"Flynn's." Johnny examined the arm Flynn stretched out to him but spotted nothing of interest. "Daddy."

"That's right," Flynn agreed. "Are you ready for breakfast?"

Pride came awake with a start. "Johnny?"

"He's awake and wanting to know where everybody is," Flynn said. "We have a busy day ahead of us, so let's get moving."

With that, Flynn set the pattern for the next two weeks. During the day, he escorted Pride and Johnny through houses and apartments then he took them to a museum or another attraction sure to appeal to Johnny.

At night, he either took them someplace to eat then back to his apartment, or if Pride insisted, he drove them back to Anahuac and spent the night with them. First, he told himself, Pride needed to grow accustomed to his presence. Then she might be willing to marry him.

Bettricia Sutherland got busy and located a house in a quiet suburb of Houston that she thought would be the perfect home for a young family, and Flynn lost no time in taking Pride to look at the property.

"It's not on the market yet," he told her. "The family is transferring to Dallas. If you like it, we can get the jump on everyone else."

Pride studied the spreading lawn, neat flowerbeds, and sheltering pin oak trees. "It's very nice."

"There's an above-ground swimming pool and a deck in back," he added. "It's a big backyard."

Accompanied by the homeowners, Flynn marched Pride around the entire house and the large, well-landscaped backyard.

"Nice kitchen, huh?" Flynn asked.

"It's wonderful." He could not tell what she was thinking, as she kept her face arranged in calm, expressionless lines.

"Four bedrooms," Flynn pointed out. "There aren't many houses like this available with four bedrooms."

"True."

"What do you think of the yard?"

"The yard is perfect," Pride allowed.

The backyard boasted a six-foot-high brick and wrought-iron wall and could hold several children, a swing-set, and a dog with ease. The above-ground swimming pool and deck had been arranged for family living.

When he drove them home, Johnny chattered on about the swimming pool, much to Flynn's delight.

"We ought to make an offer on it," he told Pride. "It won't last long once they put it on the market."

Pride said something noncommittal and turned to adjust Johnny's car seat.

"Centrally located, too," he added. "It's only a twenty minute drive from the office."

"Assuming there's no traffic jam on your route," Pride said. "I'm not ready to make a decision about a house or apartment right now, Flynn. I still have business in Lake Charles. It's going to be a few months before I'm ready to relocate."

Flynn fell silent, thinking hard. Obviously, he needed another plan.

Fortunately, he had already prepared Plan B.

*

Pride awakened alone in her own bed in her father's house in Anahuac. After leaving Johnny to spend the night with Flynn's parents, she had driven home to Anahuac and told Flynn she needed time alone to work on her column. Tracy Eric had some catching up to do.

Since Flynn probably needed some time to catch up on his own work, she thought the time apart would benefit both of them. The last thing she wanted was a husband who wanted her child more than he wanted her, she reminded herself.

She felt as though things between them had rocketed out of her control, and that her excuses to avoid accepting Flynn's marriage proposal had worn thin. Either she needed to marry Flynn, or she needed to give him a solid reason why she would not.

The problem, she admitted, was that she no longer had a solid reason. Flynn had successfully demolished every one of the reasons she had clung to for so long.

Somehow, she made it through the night. Unused to being alone, she kept waking up to go check Johnny's empty bed. When she awakened to check the bed beside her for Flynn, she decided it was time to get up.

She climbed out of bed and threw on her green chenille robe, smiling at her own foolishness, and wandered into the bathroom, where she scrubbed her face energetically and peered at her nose in the mirror. The hours spent in Flynn's company had exposed her to enough sun to cause her freckles to reappear. Soon, she might even develop a light tan.

With only herself to care for, Pride hardly knew how to begin the day. She stood in the kitchen a moment then settled at last on fetching the morning newspaper she had yet to cancel the subscription for. Accordingly, she opened the front door to a sparkling early summer morning.

The sun, just rising, sparkled off the dew covering the grass. Pride stood on the porch barefoot and searched the wet grass for the paper. She located it at last, hiked up her robe, and tiptoed carefully toward it.

Snatching it up by its plastic wrapper she turned to head back to the house, but the sun shone directly in her eyes and blinded her to the fact that something blocked her path. She walked into a solid male body.

"Good morning, Pride," Flynn said.

Pride gave an involuntary frightened squeak and started back. "You scared me half to death. What on earth are you doing sneaking up on me at this hour?"

"I'm glad you asked that question," Flynn said. "Have you plugged in the coffee pot, or left anything cooking?"

"Not yet." She shaded her eyes to study him.

"Wait right here."

Flynn bounded up on the porch and nipped inside the house before she could gather her wits enough to protest.

She rubbed her eyes. He wore khaki trousers, a knit polo shirt, and boat moccasins, exactly as he had when he went sailing.

Moments later, he reappeared, carting her purse and her laptop computer tote. He locked the door carefully behind him.

Pride watched him, baffled. "What are you doing?"

"I'm abducting you," Flynn said gravely.

"Oh, yes? Well, let me tell you something, Flynn. I'm not at my best at an early hour of the morning. If you expect me to be abducted or anything else at this hour, you're crazy."

"Darling, the idea of an abduction is that the abductee has no choice in the matter."

He reached her side, swept her up in his arms, newspaper and all, and walked across the wet lawn with her.

Across the street, old Mrs. Jones, in her bathrobe and slippers, watched from her porch.

Pride began to feel concerned and a little annoyed. "Put me down, Flynn Sutherland. This is not funny."

"In an abduction, the man is supposed to sweep the woman off her feet, preferably while she's wearing something long and trailing," he indicated her long, cotton robe, "and toss her into his carriage."

Pride glanced down the street. Flynn had parked his Bronco behind a hedge, where she couldn't see it from her front lawn.

"I'm not going anywhere at this hour," she said. "Put me down."

"Sorry, sweetie. In an abduction, the abductor ignores all the pleas of the abductee."

"Flynn, I am not pleading. I am telling you that if you don't put me down this minute, I'm going to—"

Flynn somehow opened the car door with her in his arms and tossed her and her belongings, inside. She and her belongings bounced on the seat then, Pride tried to fling herself back out the way she had entered.

"I hope you aren't going to force me to tie you up," Flynn said, mimicking an evil leer.

She attempted to force the door open far enough to let her slip out while Flynn closed it.

"This has gone beyond a joke," she said, in the same patient tones she used when Johnny back-sassed her. "I want you to let me out of this car."

"Sorry, darling. You're now in my power."

"I'll show you power," Pride said, and tried to shove him back with the car door.

"I think you have that backwards," Flynn said, smiling tenderly at her.

The next instant, he gathered her in his arms, pushed her further into the Bronco, and pulled out her seat belt. He locked it around her then he slammed and locked the door on her.

Pride, after a bemused second, fumbled for the seat belt release with one hand and the door lock with the other. She could locate neither immediately and lost precious seconds while Flynn rushed around and leaped into the seat beside her.

"Too late," he cried, obviously enjoying himself.

"Flynn Sutherland, if you don't stop this nonsense this instant..." Her words faded out when Flynn started the car. "What do you think you're doing?"

The Bronco leaped forward, kicking up gravel as it raced down the quiet street. Acceleration forces pushed her back against the seat.

"I keep on telling you," he said, grinning. "I'm abducting you."

"You're crazy," she said, with conviction.

"Possibly." He looked pleased with himself. "But I've thought the matter over very carefully, and this was the only viable alternative."

"Let me tell you something, Flynn Sutherland. You didn't think hard enough." She stared out the windshield, still in a state of unbelief. "As a matter of interest, what were the other alternatives?"

"The way I saw it," Flynn said, in confiding tones, "there were really only two alternatives. One, I could try to reason with you on land, and two, I could try to reason with you on the water. Naturally, great sailor that I am, I opted to reason with you at sea."

"If you think you're going to reason with me anywhere at all after this, you've finally flipped."

"I know what's wrong here," Flynn observed. "You haven't had any coffee yet."

"You're right. Maybe if I had some coffee, I wouldn't be thinking about throwing myself out of this car and taking my chances hiking through the streets in my robe."

"Forget it, darling." Flynn glanced at her, brown eyes merry and admiring. "It's a nice robe, but not quite the thing for street wear."

She looked down at herself. No doubt about it, the green chenille robe looked exactly like what it was, a bathrobe.

They passed a fast food restaurant that did a brisk breakfast business. Flynn whirled the Bronco into the parking lot and turned off the motor.

"You need some breakfast," he said, in sympathetic tones. "I'll be right back."

This was her chance to leap out and telephone a taxi. Instead, Pride sat still. Several early risers sat in booths by the windows, and other cars came and went. There was no sense in giving everyone fuel for gossip. Besides, she really needed coffee.

Plus, Flynn could see her from inside the restaurant, and she saw that he kept a close eye on her.

Moments later, he returned. The fragrance of fresh perked coffee reached her nostrils, along with the appetizing smell of a take-out breakfast carton.

He handed her a plastic coffee cup, and Pride sipped it gratefully. "Maybe now I'll get some sense out of you," he said, grinning.

"I doubt it." Pride sipped more coffee. "How's Johnny this morning?"

"Still sleeping, I hope. Mom and Dad kept him up way past his bedtime last night, and he loved it."

"I'll bet he did." Pride had expected that. "I'm going to have a heck of a time getting him back on his schedule."

"You're right," Flynn said, chuckling. "I'm afraid I stayed until they put him to bed, which increased his excitability quotient. He's quite a boy, Pride."

She couldn't hide her joy in hearing others agree with her assessment of her son. "Yes, he is, isn't he? He's the only person in the world who's more stubborn than you are."

"That bad?" He smiled tenderly at her. "Are you, by any chance, hoping to beat the stubbornness out of him at a young age?"

"Of course I am," she returned. "God forbid that some young woman in the future should have to go through what I did to get my point across."

"Poor Johnny," Flynn murmured.

"Poor young woman, if I'm not successful," Pride corrected.

She examined the carton Flynn had placed on the seat beside her. It contained biscuits, scrambled eggs, and bacon, and it smelled like heaven. She shucked the wrapper off the package of plastic utensils and dug in.

"You've done a remarkable job with Johnny," Flynn said. "For all his stubbornness, you've managed to teach him manners."

"I've watched Gloria," Pride said, in dismissive tones. "She's a world-class expert in child-rearing." She grinned. "But even Gloria says Johnny is going to need extra discipline if he isn't to turn out like you."

"Is that so? It's a good thing you've introduced him to me, isn't it? I can help you bear the burden of the extra discipline."

"Now that I've introduced him to you, that's exactly what you're going to do." Pride chewed a crisp slice of bacon in a reflective way. "I'll start keeping a chart as soon as he's old enough to understand. Every time he's bad, I'll enter a black mark on the chart. When you get him, you'll be expected to apply discipline for each and every black mark."

Flynn glanced at her. "That's rough. The poor kid will dread seeing me."

"No, he won't. You'll find Johnny is always determined that *this* time he's going to get away with something."

"Oh."

"I have a feeling your mother can tell you something about that." The prospect cheered Pride considerably.

"I guess there's only one thing I can do, since you're obviously going to refuse to be reasonable about this," Flynn said thoughtfully.

"What's that?" She sipped more coffee.

"I'll have to continue with the abduction."

An abduction didn't sound quite so bad, now that she'd had coffee and food. "I'd rather go back home, if you don't mind. I still have to get my column into final form, and email it to the newspaper—"

"Pride, darling, abductors don't ask the abductee's blessing on the abduction."

Pride gathered her utensils, coffee cup, and empty food carton back into the paper sack. "May I ask why you find it necessary to abduct me?"

"It's quite simple, darling." He smiled at her. "I'm going to see to it that there's nothing to distract you while you consider my proposal."

Chapter Eleven

Pride rode halfway to Galveston in a state of bewildered disbelief. At any moment, Flynn would say he was teasing and turn the car around. Surely he wasn't taking her sailing in her robe and nightie.

She ignored his mention of a proposal. Whatever it was, she didn't think she wanted to know.

Flynn didn't press her. He maintained a flow of small talk about Johnny's antics the night before and his parents' response to them. The elder Sutherlands felt they were dealing with a young Flynn all over again. They appeared both enchanted and frightened by the prospect.

"By the way," Flynn said, in casual tones. "They'll be keeping him for the next few days."

Pride stared at his profile a moment but couldn't think of anything adequate to say.

By the time the Bronco approached the causeway that led directly into Galveston, Pride had recovered herself.

"This really isn't funny, Flynn. If you wanted to go sailing or something, you could have given me a few minutes to shower and put on some clothes."

"No problem," Flynn said, with a gesture that indicated the rear of the vehicle. "I've packed everything you're likely to need."

"You've what?"

She twisted to look over her shoulder. Flynn had packed the rear of the vehicle with totes and plastic bags.

"How long are you planning on staying out?" she asked.

"As long as it takes," Flynn vowed.

Pride developed a fatalistic feeling about her chances of emailing her column to the *Chronicle* that morning.

She fell silent as Flynn turned down the familiar street leading to the marina. Planning what she was going to say to convince him to take her back home after a few hours spent sailing took all her concentration.

Flynn parked the car, and Pride noted that he had parked in almost the same—no, *exactly* the same—spot she had parked three years ago when she had awaited his return. Every muscle in her face and body felt frozen as she turned her head to look at Flynn. Nausea, hot and roiling, struck with a vengeance.

He unsnapped his seat belt and came to her, wrapping her in his arms.

"I realize I'll never be able to completely undo the damage I did to your heart," he said, holding her. "If I can just convince you that I hurt myself as much as I hurt you, maybe you'll give me another chance at loving you."

Pride sat very still. If she didn't move, perhaps she wouldn't upchuck her entire breakfast.

Flynn rubbed her back with his warm hands, and his breath stirred the hair at her temples. After several minutes, her tempestuous emotions grew calmer and the nausea lessened. She tried to straighten away from him.

"Hold still, darling," he said gently. "Let me hold you a moment. Did you think I wouldn't remember how you waited here for me all day, and the things I said to you when you tried to talk to me?"

She drew in a sharp, painful breath and tried to stop the tears that flooded her eyes. "Let me go, Flynn."

He touched his lips to her forehead. "I'll never let you go again. You may refuse to forgive me, but you're going to belong to me."

The tears vanished beneath the force of the anger that flooded her being. She shoved hard at his chest and succeeded in pushing him about six inches away.

"That's what you think, Flynn Sutherland. There is no way I'm going to marry you if you abduct me like this. Do you hear that?"

Flynn chuckled and wrapped her in his arms once more. Pride felt like a small, yapping dog enveloped in the arms of a friendly giant.

"I hear you," Flynn said. "However, I'm ignoring you."

"Why am I not surprised?" Pride grumbled.

Flynn laughed and reached across her to open the car door.

"Get your purse and your newspaper," he said. "You look like a person who's needed a vacation for a long time."

She couldn't think of anything bad enough to say to him. Worse, if she didn't keep her thoughts even and her body still, the nausea worsened.

He unsnapped her seat belt, lifted her onto his lap then stepped out with her riding high in his arms.

"Flynn, put me back in the car. I don't want to go sailing."

"You don't want to marry me, either," Flynn pointed out. "But I'm ignoring you. Besides, as it happens, we aren't going sailing."

"Then what are we doing here?"

"We're going yachting. My new boat awaits."

"You bought that boat?" Pride shut up a moment, digesting this. "I get it. You're marrying me for my money."

"Right. The first payment comes due in a month. Do you think we can speed up the wedding so you can give me access to your account in time—?"

Pride struck his shoulder with her fist then had to lie very still in his arms in order to avoid losing her breakfast.

Flynn laughed heartily as he carried her across the lot and walked down the wooden dock. She might have weighed nothing, judging from his free and easy stride.

Pride twisted in his arms and saw the large, blue and white motor yacht already waiting at the dock. The name caught her eye, and she gasped.

"Farah" had become "Sutherland's Pride."

"Did you ever find out who Farah was?" she asked, in her blandest tones.

"Don't ask."

Pride gulped back another upsurge of nausea and looked around for help as Flynn started up the boarding ladder with her in his arms. "Flynn, I do not wish to ride on this boat. Take me home immediately."

"Sorry, darling." He didn't sound sorry. "It isn't every woman who gets a yacht named after her. The least you can do is sanctify her launching with your presence."

"I'll sanctify it from the dock with a champagne bottle if you like." She added, "Kindly leave me your car keys."

Flynn hopped on deck and started toward the companionway, where he had to set her down to fish in his pocket for the keys so he could unlock the hatch.

Pride glanced around. The dock wasn't active yet, but already men were unloading the paper sacks from Flynn's Bronco. She stared, amazed. Moments ago, she had spotted no one on the dock.

Flynn had obviously laid his plans in advance. It looked as though the entire staff of the marina was cooperating with him. In another few moments, the men would board the boat with every one of Flynn's totes and bags.

She had to do something fast, but her only two choices seemed to involve either a major hissy-fit or tossing her entire breakfast.

Before she could embark on either course of action, Flynn lifted her in his arms once more and carried her down the companionway and into the spacious cabin. He didn't put her down until he had reached the aft stateroom, the boat's master bedroom, where he set her gently on the bed.

She heard sounds on deck, indicating that the men had boarded with Flynn's supplies. Her chance for escape was probably gone, if it had ever existed, she admitted to herself drily.

"Make yourself comfortable, darling," Flynn said, smiling tenderly. "This is your bedroom for the duration."

Her thoughts must have been obvious, judging from the way he laughed.

"No, I'm not going to force you to sleep with me," he said. "I'm hoping you'll invite me to your bed of your own free will. Why don't you take a shower and wake up a little more? I'll bring your clothes in shortly."

Pride watched as he went swiftly out, closing the door behind him. The moment he disappeared, she leaped up and ran to the head, where she lost her coffee and her breakfast.

She rinsed her mouth and washed her face while she reviewed everything she had eaten the day before. Nothing struck her as suspicious, but who knew these days? On the other hand, maybe she had the twenty-four-hour virus. If she had a virus, Flynn would have no choice but to return her to shore.

She lay down on the bed and monitored the state of her stomach closely, but the nausea seemed to have eased, so Pride arose and looked around the luxurious bedroom. The room was ringed with short curtains which covered the portholes. She pulled them aside until she located a porthole and peered out. All she could see was the opposite side of the dock, where nothing was going on at the moment. She returned to the head and turned on the shower.

While she stood beneath the warm spray, the boat began to vibrate as the powerful motor switched on. By the time she got out of the shower, Flynn would probably have her almost a mile or two out in the Gulf of Mexico.

She took her time in the shower.

When she emerged from the head, a grand total of four plastic sacks had appeared on the bed. Pride unpacked them, conscious of feeling like a child tearing into a present.

Flynn had apparently gone out the night before and bought every item of clothing he thought she'd need for a stay on the boat. Even the underwear was in perfect taste, and, she noted, in the correct sizes.

She had two swimsuits, one a blue tank suit, and the other, a hot pink bikini. She could choose among shorts, blouses and trousers. He'd even included shoes, from flip-flops to a pair of the latest, high-tech deck shoes.

She chose a pair of white shorts and a colorful, striped blouse, and tied on the deck shoes. They all fit perfectly, a testimonial to Flynn's observational powers. *When he cared to use them*, she added, reminding herself that he had missed identifying Johnny for a couple of days.

Her purse, laptop tote and her newspaper lay on the bed also. Pride automatically stowed the purse in a drawer and placed the newspaper on one of the bedside tables. She made short work of unpacking the sacks into the drawers and the wonderful, walk-in locker.

In fact, she told herself as she brushed out her hair, there was only one thing Flynn had forgotten.

"There's only one thing you forgot," she said, straight-faced, after climbing up to join Flynn in the cockpit where Flynn steered a careful course from the yacht basin toward the open Gulf of Mexico.

He lifted his sunglasses to eye her trim figure, grinning. "What's that?"

"Makeup."

"Try the medicine cabinet in the head," Flynn said, equally straight-faced.

It was too much. Pride rose from the chair she'd taken beside Flynn's helm chair and climbed back down.

In her stateroom, she went to the head and opened the medicine cabinet. Sure enough, he'd stocked it with the brand of makeup she'd been fond of three years ago. There was even a bottle of the perfume that had been his favorite.

Pride made use of the supplies and returned to the navigation station. Makeup went a long way toward making a woman feel able to face a difficult situation.

She glanced around, trying to estimate their distance from the shore.

"We're about a mile out," Flynn said. "With a motor yacht, I don't have the right-of-way anymore."

"Great. I should be able to swim to shore."

"Why would you want to do that?" he asked, looking hurt. "Have you looked in the refrigerator? We've got enough food for an army. You're going to cook me one of your fantastic on-board lunches."

"Flynn, it's time you understood something."

"What's that?" His glance was innocent in the extreme.

"I have been kidnapped onto this boat. I did not come aboard of my own free will. Therefore, I refuse to cook."

"The skipper of the boat assigns the duties," Flynn informed her. "Anyone refusing to carry out said duties will be keelhauled."

"Keelhaul away, then, because I am not cooking."

"You'll get awfully hungry."

"Maybe I'll starve to death. You can toss my body overboard and let the sharks have me."

"Pride."

"Yes, Flynn?"

"You have a son to think about."

"Poor Johnny." She added in sorrowful tones, "Poor, little, motherless boy."

"Pride."

"Yes, Flynn?"

"Don't."

He was serious, she saw. Pride shut up and hid her smile.

Flynn slowed the boat to yield the right of passage to a ketch under sail. He kept his gaze fixed straight ahead, which was a good thing since their passage was cluttered by other boats.

Pride stood and walked around the small enclosure, studying the white, cushioned benches placed for the comfort of guests.

She came back to examine the electronic gadgets the helm was equipped with, many of them things Flynn had talked about for years.

She climbed back onto the chair beside Flynn's. "What are we going to do on this boat?"

"What do you mean?" He glanced at her. "It should be obvious that this is a pleasure boat."

"That's just it," Pride pointed out. "About this time on your sloop, we'd be hauling down the jib and hoisting something else in its place. You'd be running around tightening this and loosening that, and tacking first this way, then that way. What are we going to do if you don't have to sail?"

"We're going to talk."

That's what she was afraid of.

"I'm better at writing," she said. "Why don't you submit your questions and subjects for discussion then let me retire to my cabin and type up some answers? I've got my laptop, so you'll get a lot more food for thought if I can write than you will if you want to listen to me waffle around."

"I'd rather listen to you waffle around, thank you." Flynn smiled at her. "Go below, darling. You've been in the sun long enough."

Pride looked at him in disbelief.

"Either that, or put on a hat," Flynn added. "I'm not having you sunburned or sick the first day out."

He was right, she acknowledged. It was all too easy to sit in the breeze and be deceived about the sun's burning power as the early morning sun climbed higher in the sky. Soon, it would be midday, and her fair skin would be most vulnerable. With an envious glance at Flynn's dark tan, Pride went below.

She went through the salon and into the white Formica-covered galley. She was almost tempted to start something cooking when she studied the conveniently located appliances.

Opening the refrigerator and the cabinets, Pride marveled at the way Flynn had packed in groceries of every conceivable kind. He was right. They had enough supplies to keep them in luxury for a good two weeks at sea.

She shut the cabinets and stalked toward her cabin. She didn't have two weeks to dawdle around at sea. She had a son to take care of and article deadlines, not to mention the Tracy Eric column, which should have her editor at the *Chronicle* very nervous by this hour.

She located a hat, jammed it on her head, and stalked back up to the nav station, where Flynn, bare-headed and magnificently male after shedding his knit shirt, enjoyed his new purchase.

"Flynn, I can't stay out here longer than this afternoon," she began, without preamble.

"Sure, you can," Flynn said. "In fact, you'd better plan on it."

"My column has to be in by noon today at the very latest," she argued. "It's supposed to run tomorrow. They're holding space—"

"Then you'd better go finish it up, hadn't you?" Flynn asked, unperturbed. "We have Wi-Fi, so all you have to do is hit the 'send' key."

First, she had to finish the column.

Steaming gently, Pride went to her cabin, set up her laptop, and read over what she had written. It detailed her son's introduction to his father and his father's reactions to her son's antics. She would be the first to admit the column skimmed neatly over the deeper emotions, but at the moment, she felt she simply could not do them justice.

However, her editor, Christi Dumont, thought the column would do very well.

"The readers will love it," Christi wrote in a return email. "They're all romantics at heart, and your column right now is just like a soap opera."

"He'll be lucky if I don't strangle him," Pride wrote back.

"If you kill him, I want to be the first person notified. And if you wind up marrying him, I want Tracy Eric to go out in glory," Christi returned.

Pride fought off the urge to break her laptop over Flynn's head. She went instead to the cabin and placed a phone call to her cousin Gloria.

"You're *where*?" Gloria asked.

"You heard me. He says he's abducted me, and I'm stranded somewhere in the middle of the Gulf of Mexico. Tonight I think I'll steal the dinghy and row to shore."

"Are you kidding?" Gloria said. "Stay out there and have it out with him. It looks like he's in the mood to listen to you at last. You might as well take advantage of it."

"That's a misconception if there ever was one. Nothing has changed. He's still ignoring my feelings. He didn't even ask if I wanted to go boating. He just grabbed me and hauled me out here."

"I don't think he's ignoring your feelings," Gloria said thoughtfully. "I think *you're* ignoring your feelings. Why don't you try listening with your heart instead of your ears, for once? I think you'll find out that Flynn was as hurt as you were."

Pride breathed fire. "I'll listen to Flynn exactly the way he listened to me three years ago."

"You're still holding on to the bitterness and hurt of the past. Don't let it cost you your chance at happiness."

"What makes you think Flynn Sutherland is my only chance at happiness?" Pride demanded. "There are other men out there, you know."

"So how many of them have you been out with in the past two years?"

"Just because I've been too busy to date much—"

"Don't hand me that. I heard what you had to say about all three of them. It was perfectly clear that you were comparing them to Flynn and they were coming up short. Wise up, Pride. You have a heaven-sent opportunity. Don't muff it while you keep waiting for him to turn into your father."

Pride replaced the receiver and huffed out a breath. She should have known better than to call Gloria.

The person she really wanted to call was Johnny, but since she lacked the Sutherlands' phone number and she didn't want to go up and talk to Flynn again, that was out of the question.

She went to the aft deck and sat on one of the comfortable chairs in the shade. There, she watched the shore recede until it was no longer visible on the horizon, and she began to see fewer and fewer boats.

She was tired, she realized suddenly.

Tired of fighting, tired of being strong, tired of pretending single motherhood was a piece of cake. She dozed, pleasantly lethargic, awakened and dozed again.

The sun rode at high noon by the time she heard the big motor cut off. Moments later, she heard Flynn's footsteps.

"I thought you'd have lunch going by now," he said, casting himself into a chair beside her.

Pride didn't feel called upon to answer him. She merely raised her brows and continued to gaze out over the water.

"Pride," he said gently, "I don't blame you for being mad at me. I've behaved like a prize ass." He paused, but she said nothing. "Aren't you going to agree with me?"

"What for?" she asked. "Facts are facts." She turned to face him. "I want to go home, Flynn."

"You shall, but not right away."

She came to a gentle boil at this expert application of heat. "When?"

He smiled. "I don't think you want to hear the answer to that."

"Probably not, but when?"

"I'll take you home just as soon as you agree to my proposal."

"And what, please, is your proposal?"

"It's really quite simple. All I want is what I should have had three years ago—you."

"You had me three years ago, Flynn. You just didn't want me." She propped her chin on her hand and stared at the water. "The fact that you're willing to propose now says it all as far as I'm concerned."

"It does, indeed," Flynn agreed. "I'm proposing now because I've gone three years without you, and life has been pure hell."

Pride stared at the water and said nothing. If Flynn had really wanted her, she had been easy enough to locate. He was just trying to talk her into marrying him so he could have easy access to Johnny.

"What will it take to convince you I'm serious?"

"I have no idea. I've told you, I'm moving back to Houston. You can see Johnny every day if you want to. I'm not going to be doing things to circumvent your rights as a father. Can't you let it go at that? You don't have to be married to me to have free access to your son."

"I'm not talking about Johnny," Flynn said. "I'm talking about us. You and me. I want you to be my wife. I want the woman I love with me again, the way it used to be."

"She doesn't exist anymore," Pride said. "People change in three years, Flynn. I'm not as trusting or as hopeful as I used to be."

"I've noticed. What you're really saying is that you don't trust me."

"All I'm saying is that I'm a different person now. If you got to know me, you'd probably change your mind about wanting to marry me."

Flynn smiled and leaned forward. "That's why you're here. I'm going to get to know you again."

*

Flynn watched Pride pick at the plate of hot tamales he served her for supper and wondered if he had gone too far by hauling Pride out on the high seas for negotiations. Rather than berate him, or try to get him to return her to shore, she had chosen to sit in lethargic silence on the aft deck most of the afternoon, gazing out over the water.

He had anchored the boat far out in the Gulf, with no other vessels in sight. But he had yet to engage Pride in any sort of meaningful conversation.

"Is something wrong with the tamales?" he asked.

"They're fine. I'm just not very hungry." She nibbled a bite of tamale. "I was sick this morning, and I'm still not too sure of my stomach's status, so I'm being very careful."

"You were sick? Why didn't you tell me?"

He studied her pale face and too-slim figure. Pride needed a long rest, but making her take one required major coercion. He wondered how to get it across to her that she was on vacation.

"All it involved was a little nausea. Once I threw up, everything was okay." She shrugged. "I thought it might be a virus, but whatever it was, it seems to be over."

He watched her with concern. "When was the last time you had a vacation?"

She said nothing and cast him a sardonic glance.

"That's what I thought. You need a keeper, Pride Donovan, and I'm taking on the job."

"What has catching a virus got to do with a vacation?" Pride wanted to know. "When there's a child in the house, especially one who attends preschool or daycare, viruses flow through the house in a steady stream. You should hear some of the things my readers tell me."

"You need more rest," Flynn said. "Your immune system is probably down."

She gave him a frustrated look and ate a tamale in a defiant way. "In that case, don't look for me to cook you a good breakfast in the morning. I'm going to be sleeping late."

"Fine. I can see I didn't abduct you a minute too soon," he said. "You're going to bed early tonight."

Pride ate a piece of lettuce leaf. "There's nothing wrong with me, but I have no objections. Especially if it gets me out of washing dishes."

"I don't think I'm going to allow you to do anything. You've been going at ninety miles an hour for the past three years, haven't you?"

She shot him a suspicious look. "I've been busy, yes. With a baby on the way and a living to earn, I couldn't afford to sit around much."

"Those days are over." On that Flynn had decided. "So get used to it."

Pride gave him the first real grin he had seen that day. "If you insist."

"I do."

"Then would you mind signing a little note to that effect?" She gave him a melting look. "In blood, and in triplicate, please."

Satisfied, he grinned back. "Anything you like, darling."

Chapter Twelve

Flynn sat on the aft deck and watched the moon cast a lighted lane across the dark Gulf waters. Ordinarily, he never second-guessed himself, but this occasion was an exception. He had screwed up royally in regard to Pride, and he feared his efforts to mend the situation might wind up in the screw-up bin also.

He wondered briefly why he had believed Pride would be easier to reason with if he brought her out on the Gulf on his new boat. It was becoming more and more obvious that Pride considered the action another attempt to override her wishes and rob her of her right to choose.

He smiled grimly. It was, of course, but he had hoped she wouldn't notice that.

No doubt he had gone flat out crazy. If he had any sense, he would take her back to shore first thing tomorrow morning.

He sighed and leaned forward, balancing his elbows on his knees. All his instincts urged him to grab her and make her his without delay. Unfortunately, Pride had other ideas, although he had no idea what they were. All he knew was that they didn't seem to include him.

She had insisted on talking to Johnny before she went to bed, and he had obligingly called his parents. They were, he learned, quite thrilled with Pride's last "Single Mommy" column, which examined her feelings upon introducing her son to his paternal grandparents.

He had read the column also, but what he derived from it was the tremendous sense of relief Pride felt at knowing her son had grandparents he could love, and who would step in if something happened to her.

Tracy Eric said very little about the reappearance of her "former lover." In fact, she seemed to be going out of her way to avoid discussing him.

Pride would sleep with him, go out with him and spend time with him and Johnny as a family, but she avoided all talk of marriage and she refused to write a word about her feelings for him. If she still had any.

Maybe he should find out more about Pride's plans for the future. Then he could work on convincing her that he could safely be included.

On that thought, he rose and turned to head inside. Pride, wearing only a short pink nightgown, stood in the hatchway, watching him.

"What is it, darling?" Maybe he could begin now to find out what was on her mind.

"I was just wondering when you were coming to bed." She held out her hand to him. "Is everything all right?"

His spirits promptly shot into the stratosphere. She wanted him sexually. That was something.

"Everything's fine, darling." He took her hand. "I'm coming now."

He followed her below and turned her into his arms the moment they stepped over the threshold into the master cabin.

Tomorrow he would talk with Pride about her plans and how he could fit himself into them.

Tonight, he concentrated on loving her with everything at his command. Maybe she would feel his love for her in the way he caressed and kissed her. She belonged to him, and one way or another, Flynn intended to prove it.

*

Pride awakened alone much later than she usually awakened. She lay still for a moment in an attempt to orient herself, but nothing helped. She felt dizzy and nauseous and could not seem to get her bearings.

She sat up, only to lie down again with a moan of misery. The virus still had her in its grip, and in order to feel better, she would probably have to die.

Either that or throw up. She flung the covers off and sat on the edge of the bed just as Flynn entered.

He wore only a pair of swimming trunks and carried a tray of food. Pride noted that he looked like everything she had ever wanted, tall and solidly male.

Then she saw the plate of scrambled eggs, bacon and toast. Her stomach gave a mighty heave and she launched herself toward the head and prayed to make it in time.

For the next few minutes she noticed nothing except the insurrection in her stomach, but as the storm began to wind down, she grew conscious of Flynn holding her steady and patting her face with a wet washcloth.

"You're still sick." He lifted her in his arms and carried her back to the bed. "I'd better get you back to shore. You need to see a doctor."

"Maybe you'd better," she said, in a weak voice. "Johnny hasn't been sick, so I have no idea what I've been exposed to."

"You don't feel feverish." He pulled the covers over her. "Lie still, darling. I'll get the boat underway. We should be back at the marina by this afternoon."

Pride frowned and kept her eyes closed. "I'm sorry about this, Flynn. I don't know what's wrong with me."

"How do you feel now?"

"Still queasy, but better, I think." She opened her eyes. "I'd better not try and eat that nice breakfast you cooked."

"Don't even think about it." He smoothed her hair back from her face. "Don't worry about anything, Pride. Just rest."

At the moment, that was all she felt capable of. Flynn left the room, taking her breakfast with him. She felt marginally better, but not well enough to contemplate bacon and eggs.

A few moments later, she felt the boat quiver and heard the powerful motor kick on. Knowing Flynn, he had probably already called ahead and arranged for her to see a doctor the minute he got her back to land.

After spending about half an hour lying in bed, Pride finally rose and dressed in a pair of shorts and a loose cotton blouse. Her stomach felt a little shaky, but nothing major seemed wrong with her, so she brushed her hair out and applied a little makeup, then peered at her reflection in the mirror.

She looked completely normal. Usually, when she was sick, she looked as if she had been socked in both eyes. Maybe she needed to call Flynn's parents for an update on Johnny's condition, just in case Johnny began showing symptoms.

Rather than go above deck and join Flynn in the cockpit, she gathered her belongings and stowed them in her laptop tote. She felt a twinge of annoyance when her fingers touched the crackle of the envelope her father had left her. She had stuffed it into the bottom of her tote on the principle of "out of sight, out of mind."

After avoiding the envelope for the past few weeks in favor of being with Flynn and Johnny, maybe she should go ahead and read it.

Not that she wanted to, Pride thought, plucking it from her tote with two fingers. She felt sure she did not want to read or otherwise know about whatever it contained. She extracted the old letter her mother had written to her father and opened it in the manner of one fearful of finding a poisonous snake inside.

The date on the envelope signified the letter had been written almost a year before Pride had been born, and nearly three months before the couple's wedding. The envelope appeared to have been sprinkled liberally with water drops.

Cold with dread, Pride unfolded the enclosed letter on the coffee table. It, also, looked as though it had been left out in a rain shower.

I've received the money you sent, her mother wrote. *But I can't do it. This is our baby! Isn't there some other way? I don't mind leaving school and getting a job. What does it matter if we marry a little earlier than we planned? Come to me this weekend, my darling. We need to talk more before we do something so irrevocable.*

Understanding, Pride closed her eyes, filled with sorrow. The few sentences in the letter explained everything that had puzzled her throughout her childhood, just as Alan Donovan must have known they would.

She slowly refolded the letter and returned it to the envelope. Her father had methodically discarded all her mother's letters and other keepsakes, but he had held onto this one. Pride wondered why, and decided he had probably kept it for exactly this purpose.

Twenty years, she thought, and shook her head. For twenty years, her parents had punished each other because of the termination of an unplanned pregnancy. Her mother punished her father by withholding her love and physical passion. Her father had retaliated by denigrating his wife in public and claiming Pride was not his child.

Pride realized now that her gentle mother, rather than risk standing her ground and having the child on her own, had given in to ending the pregnancy. In retaliation, she withdrew her love, even though she went ahead with the marriage.

Pride had decided early that if Flynn could not accept that he had fathered her child, she would never marry him. Maybe her subconscious had picked up on her parents' signals and had adjusted her own outlook early.

She tried to ignore the persistent thought that Flynn knew Johnny was his, that Flynn was obviously thrilled with Johnny. What if he pretended to believe her in order to provide his parents with a grandchild?

On that note, she clapped her hand over her eyes. Flynn was no actor, and she certainly couldn't see him putting on a pretense for any such reason. Perhaps she was losing it.

Pride left the bedroom and climbed slowly to the deck, where she sat down at the rail and stared out over the gleaming green waters of the Gulf. Her own problem remained, namely, how to convince Flynn that he didn't have to marry her in order to have access to Johnny.

She wasn't her mother. She could rear Johnny on her own if she had to. She did not need a husband who didn't want her.

But Flynn did want her. Everything he said and did proclaimed that fact. All she had to do was take him up on it.

Her thoughts continued in circles for the time she sat there contemplating the water and the unending horizon.

The boat plowed across a series of waves, and Pride's stomach protested. Rather than take any chances, she went below to stare at herself in the mirror over the sink once more.

She felt really weird. Sick, yet not sick. In fact, she remembered feeling like this once before in her life....

Pride's eyes rounded with shock. Electrified, she gripped the sink and counted back.

Her thoughts bounced this way and that, between disbelief and joy, then anger, then back to disbelief. Only one thing seemed clear in the morass of tangled emotions that swirled through her. She wanted to kill Flynn Sutherland.

She paced the room, alternately laughing and shaking with a strange kind of fury. Whoever had said lightning never struck twice in the same place was an idiot and a liar.

She stared down at her currently flat abdomen. Maybe she was wrong. Maybe she really did have a virus.

But before the thoughts fully formed in her mind, she knew the truth. She was not sick at all. She was pregnant.

Again.

And it was all Flynn's fault.

She thought about climbing up to the cockpit and braining him with the nearest hard object.

She sat down on the bed. On second thought, that would be too easy. What Flynn needed was a much more serious expression of her thoughts on the subject. The only problem was, she couldn't think of anything bad enough to do to him.

During the three hours it took Flynn to bring the boat back to shore, Pride considered and discarded about a dozen scenarios. Nothing seemed to fit the occasion properly.

This time, she told herself, Flynn would either do the right thing or she really would break her laptop computer over his head.

For some reason, that thought calmed her chaotic thoughts instantly. She went to the walk-in closet and picked through the clothing Flynn had furnished her and finally settled on a pair of navy-blue shorts and a blouse that looked amazingly similar to an outfit she had worn almost three years ago.

She waited until she felt the boat power down then watched out the port hole as Flynn guided the boat into the marina and docked at his slip. While he went through the process of docking at the other side of the boat, she rushed on deck and hopped down the boarding ladder and onto the dock.

The boardwalk of the marina had long been familiar to her. She hurried down it to the parking lot and walked toward Flynn's Bronco, which still sat in the same spot where she had awaited him three years ago. Once she reached it, she turned back and stared at the boat.

The moment Flynn appeared on deck, obviously in search of her, she stalked forcefully across the parking lot toward Sutherland's Pride, rocking peacefully in its slip.

Flynn stood at the deck rail watching her, just as he had three years ago. Absently, she noted that he wore a pair of khaki trousers and a white knit shirt, much as he had then.

Pride ran onto the dock, put her hands on her hips, and yelled up at him, "The problem isn't going to go away if you run from it."

From the corner of her vision, she noted the presence of a pair of dock workers, watching them with interest.

She waited, fuming. Amazingly, she found herself almost as angry as she had been three years ago. How dare Flynn do this to her again?

Flynn leaned over the deck rail, unsmiling. "Then maybe you'd better come aboard so we can discuss the matter."

What was he saying? She ran the sentence through her mental computer and came up with nothing, other than the fact that this was not what he had said three years ago.

It still wasn't what she wanted to hear. Therefore, she would have to go aboard and kill him.

He waited while she scrambled up the boarding ladder and reached out to help her step on deck. The moment her feet touched the deck, he swept her into his arms and kissed her.

"I know how to make the problem go away." He held her so tightly, she could barely breathe. "I'm going to marry you."

"Flynn, I hate to tell you this, but that will not make the problem go away," Pride said with exaggerated patience.

This was better, but she needed more.

He loosened his grip slightly and gazed thoughtfully at her face. "You're saying the problem will remain, whether we get married or not?"

"Look at Johnny." She reared back and gave him boding frown. "Would he have gone away if we had gotten married three years ago?"

"No, thank God." His mouth turned up in a huge grin. "But you might have had some help during those nights when he cried all night."

She liked this, but she wanted more. "On second thought, the problem might be considerably mitigated if we get married." She cast her gaze upwards and pretended to ponder the situation. "There's a lot to be said for shared misery and splitting the duties of childcare."

"I told you so. We'll get married next weekend. How's that? Then you can make me get up with him at night."

"We ought to make it this weekend," Pride informed him. "The sooner the better. People can count, you know."

"I'm all for that. I'll make the arrangements." Flynn regarded her with grave attention. "May I ask what changed your mind?"

He still had no clue. Pride registered that at the same time she realized that Flynn really did love her.

She gave him a bright smile. "I knew you wouldn't want a second unwed-father incident on your record. Your parents would be absolutely horrified."

"A second—?" He stopped, and a stunned look spread over his face. "Pride?"

"Like I keep on telling you, Flynn Sutherland, you need to see another doctor. I don't think there's a thing wrong with your fertility."

He stared at her a moment in silence. "I think it's more a case of finding the right, truly compatible woman." He closed his eyes then opened them again. "Are you sure?"

"Yes and no."

"What?"

The dawning look of disappointment on his face shook her.

She hastened to explain. "Yes, I'm sure, but no, I haven't run any tests. We can stop at a pharmacy and buy one of those little test kits on the way home."

Flynn lifted her off her feet and swung her around in a circle, still holding her close. "Let's do that. I can't wait to tell Dad. He won't believe it." He set her down and framed her face between his hands. "I love you, Pride. Do you believe me now?"

"I suppose I'd better," she teased, laughing at him. "Otherwise, I'll have to write a column dissecting how I let myself get seduced and pregnant again so my readers can take warning."

"Be sure and put in something flattering about my manly

charm and smooth approach." He kissed her nose. "I do love you, you know. I realized within a few weeks after you left that I was a fool to let you go."

"It doesn't matter, Flynn. We can start over again today, because I love you, too."

She meant it, she realized, surprised at herself. Some radical change had occurred inside her.

He stared at her. "You love me? Are you sure?"

"Well, now that you mention it..." She trailed off, laughing at his expression.

"Don't joke about this. It's too shattering." He held her close. "I wasn't going to give up hope, but from my point of view, things were looking pretty grim. May I ask what changed your mind?"

"I don't think anything changed my mind." Pride looked into her feelings with as much honesty as she could muster. "I knew I still loved you. I just didn't want to trust you. But I finally read the letter Daddy left me, and I realized he had reached the end of his life before he saw how different things could have been."

"What do you mean, darling," Flynn asked tenderly.

"He could have won my mother's love again, but instead, he chose to punish her by pretending he thought she was two-timing him, and she punished him by withdrawing her love. I didn't want to wind up like him, longing for forgiveness and a new start on my deathbed."

"That couldn't happen with us," Flynn said, grinning. "After all, we have Tracy Eric on our side. Eventually, she would have analyzed the situation and straightened everything out."

Pride rested her forehead on his shoulder. "I hope so, but Tracy was in over her head on this one."

"Seriously, what happens to Tracy Eric when she's no longer a single mother?"

"I don't know." She thought about it, remembering certain comments made by her editor the day before. "The way I see it, she has two choices. One, she can keep writing from a single mother's point of view and say nothing about her marriage, or two, she can end the column."

"I've become one of Tracy's main fans," Flynn protested. "She can't end her column."

"Once Tracy gets married to the father of her child, everything changes." She snuggled against him, enjoying the solid, male body and listening to his strong heartbeat. "Some things are common to all mothers, but the 'Single Mommy' column was popular because it discussed all the things married mommies usually don't have to deal with."

"Uh-oh." Flynn held her closer. "Maybe we'd better go below and discuss this. It's a scary thought that I'm messing with your career like this by marrying you."

"There are other column ideas," Pride said, smiling. "Freelance writers are adaptable. In fact, I have plans for Tracy Eric to go out with a bang."

"Oh, yes?" Flynn regarded her with trepidation. "Are you planning a big spread in the paper on our wedding or something?"

"Heavens, no. That would be my editor's province. But I'll have to tell my readers that I've fallen in love and plan to marry the father of my child, which means Tracy Eric won't be a single mommy anymore."

Flynn pulled her close for a lingering kiss. "I like that. You've fallen in love. With me. High time is all I've got to say." He swung her up in his arms and headed to the hatch. "I've never fallen out of love with you. That's why I didn't approach you at your father's funeral. I wanted you all to myself in my office the next day."

"And instead, I showed up with lots and lots of company."

"That you did." Flynn laughed and kicked the cabin door shut behind him. "It's a good thing I didn't realize at the time that Johnny was my son. I might have fainted. Killeen wouldn't have known what to do."

"Sure, she would. Everybody knows that a glass of water splashed in the face always works."

"The shock of that would compound the faint." Flynn began removing her blouse. "And Killeen would lose her Christmas bonus."

She felt his hands on her breasts and savored the sensations of cool air and warm, rough male hands gliding over her tender skin. "That would be awful. Tracy Eric's main fan, missing her Christmas bonus."

"So it's probably a good thing I didn't realize Johnny was our son until after I'd had time to adjust somewhat." He unbuttoned her shorts, skimmed them off her hips and let them drop to the floor. "Killeen's bonus is saved. But her work might suffer if her main mentor, Tracy Eric, quits writing. You'd better think of a way to keep Tracy alive and writing."

"Tracy's going to write a book," Pride murmured, not much interested at the moment. "All her fans have to do is consult the book, because everything she learned will be in it, complete with an index so they can look things up."

"That should save Killeen's sanity." Flynn lifted her and laid her on the bed then reached into his pocket for a knotted handkerchief. He carefully untied the knot and freed a ring that sparkled with green fire, which he slid gently on the ring finger of her left hand.

"In the meantime," he added, "I'll tell Mom to plan the wedding and get the house ready. We'll be married and spend our honeymoon on the boat."

"This isn't the honeymoon?"

He followed her down and stretched out beside her. "It's the first day of a long honeymoon, and you're right. It starts today."

Pride discovered she was totally in favor of that.

*

Three weeks later, Pride heard the front door of their new home open and left the kitchen, where she had been tearing lettuce for a salad, to greet Flynn in the living room.

"You're home early." She hurried to kiss him, conscious again of the thrill she felt in knowing this man loved her.

"Things at the office were in mourning today, thanks to the publication of Tracy Eric's last column. I decided the kindest thing to do was call an early halt to the misery." Flynn smiled at her. "Besides, I wanted to see what you and Johnny were up to."

"Johnny is busy with the building blocks your dad gave him. He's in the process of constructing a house for the beetle he found in the flower bed."

"Beetle? Uh-oh. You don't think he'll eat the beetle, do you?" Flynn draped his arm over her shoulders and followed her to the kitchen, where he stripped off his suit jacket and laid it over a chair back.

"I'm not allowing him to catch the beetle until he has the house built for it." She reached into the refrigerator, took out a soft drink and handed it to him. "So Killeen is upset about Tracy Eric's retirement?"

"The office is practically shrouded in black." Flynn took a swallow and set the bottle on the counter so he could unbutton his cuffs and roll up his sleeves. "She says that if Tracy's book isn't in her hands quickly, she doesn't know what will happen at her house."

"You've got your watch back." She smiled at the newly repaired mariner's watch on his left wrist. "Maybe you'd better take it off before Johnny sees it."

"Johnny has so many new toys, my watch probably won't even catch his eye any longer."

As if to give him the lie, Johnny appeared in the doorway, spotted Flynn, and came running, shouting at the top of his voice, "Flynn's. Daddy's."

When Flynn stooped to scoop up his son, the child's small fingers closed over the watch.

"Mine," Johnny said and tugged.

"Uh-oh," Flynn said. "What would Tracy Eric suggest in a case like this?"

"Tracy Eric would castigate you for continuing to wear that watch." Pride couldn't help but laugh at the sight. "She would advise you to wear that replacement watch you bought or use your cell phone like everyone else."

Flynn tried to pry Johnny's little fingers off his watch. The attempt produced a small insurrection, complete with illegal fireworks and attempts at subversion.

"What would she recommend now?" he asked.

"She'd say this is a wonderful opportunity to practice some child discipline."

"That's what I was afraid she'd say." Flynn unclasped his watch and let Johnny pull it off his wrist. "Let the poor, deprived child play with it a moment."

"Flynn," Pride began in dangerous tones.

"Just for a minute," Flynn said, chuckling. "I'll scour the stores tomorrow for a child's version of a mariner's watch."

"Failing that, Mickey Mouse will do."

"For a son of mine? Have some decency, Pride. He's got to start learning his signal flags."

They both watched as Johnny settled on the floor with the watch and began prying away at the crystal.

After a moment, Pride said, "Flynn, this would be a really good time to take that watch back."

"Look at him. He's having too much fun—hey. He got the crystal off. Johnny—"

Flynn spoke too late. Johnny popped the crystal into his mouth.

Pride moved swiftly to pry open the little mouth and extract the crystal then nabbed the watch from his hands, ignoring Johnny's wails. "This is it, Flynn Sutherland. Either you put that watch up until he's twenty, or I'll do something drastic."

Flynn put the watch and crystal in his pocket, laughing. "Sorry, son. Your mother has spoken, and in no uncertain terms."

"Daddy's," Johnny wailed. "Flynn's."

"It has to go back to the shop, I'm afraid," Flynn lifted the child and cradled him in his arms. "But don't worry. I'll get it out when you turn twenty. That's when I'll present it to you as a memento of the day I met my firstborn son." He looked at Pride. "And the day I found my heart again."

Pride returned his smile and watched as Flynn carried his son down the hall to examine the house Johnny was building. Joy washed through her in a tidal wave of feeling that never seemed to lessen, followed by gratitude that Flynn was hers again.

This time, she would never let him go.

About the Author

Kathryn Brocato was born in Texas, grew up in Arkansas and graduated from high school and college in Southeast Texas, where she and her husband, Charles, are scientists and business owners. A true believer in the happy ending, she is a lifelong reader and writer of romance.

When she is not writing, Kathryn enjoys birding, gardening, and tending her backyard chicken flock.

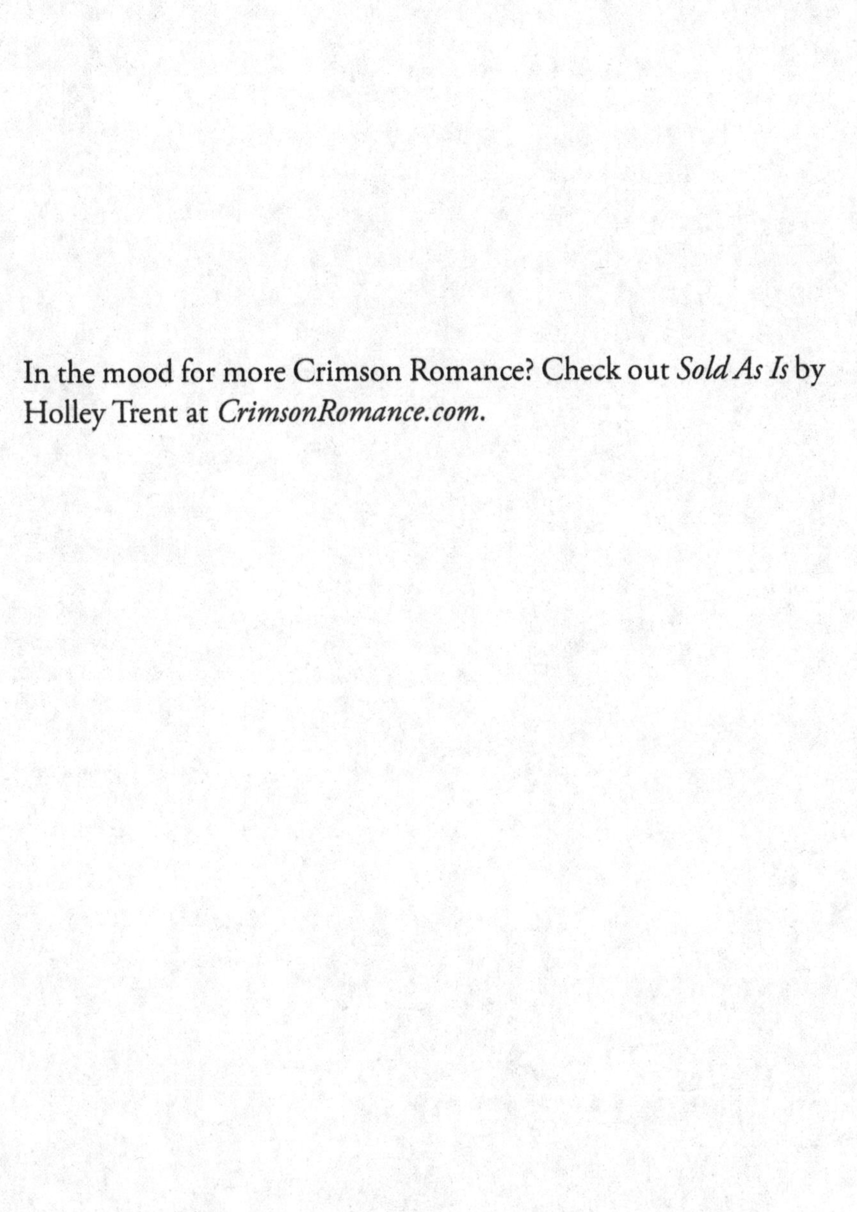

In the mood for more Crimson Romance? Check out *Sold As Is* by Holley Trent at *CrimsonRomance.com*.